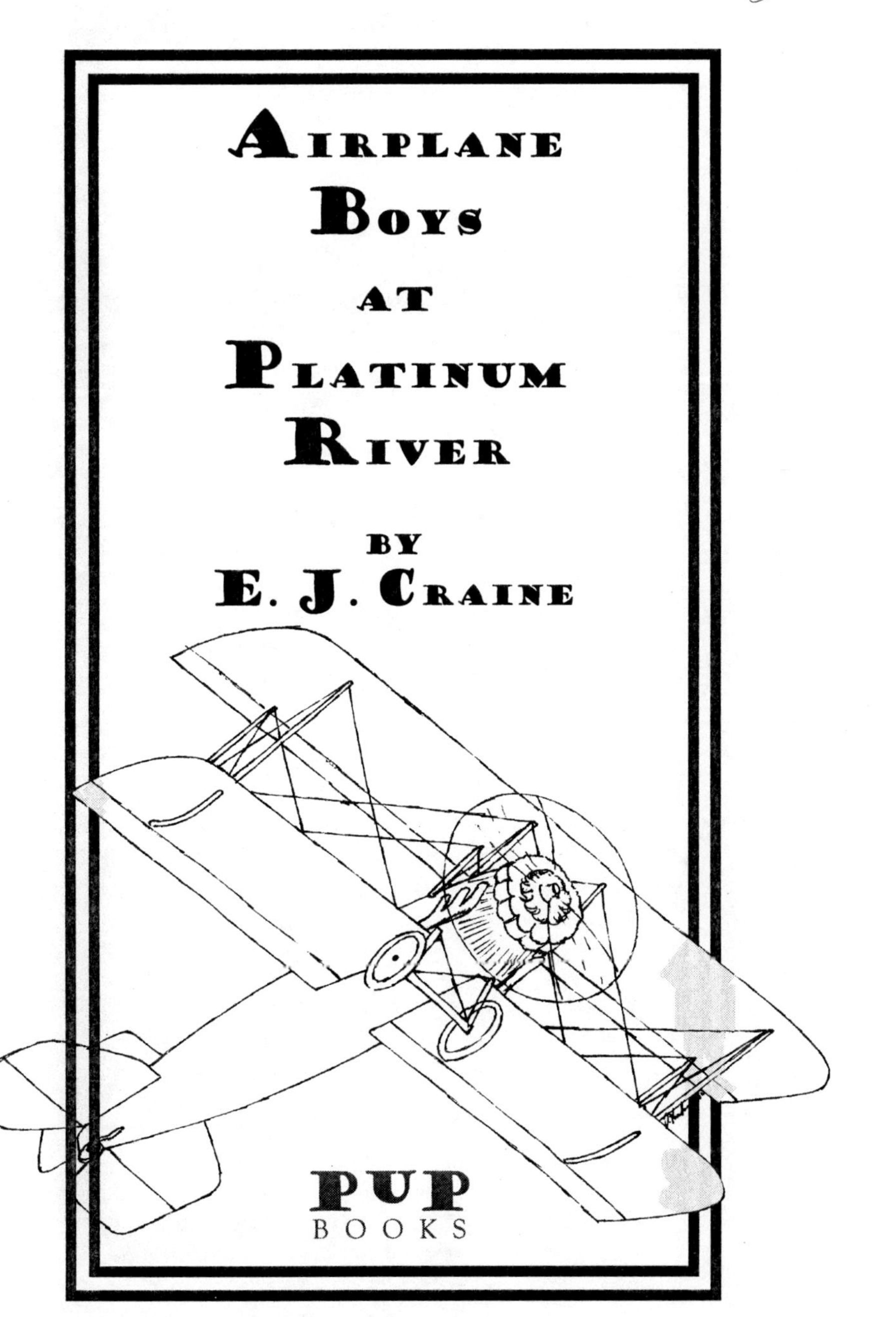

Airplane Boys at Platinum River

by

E. J. Craine

PUP BOOKS

First PuP Books Edition

2003

PuP Books is the juvenile division of
Purdue University Press

ISBN 1-55753-320-2
Printed in the United States of America

Originally Published in 1931
by
The World Syndicate Publishing Company

Cover design by Daniel C. Kirchmann

The language used in this book has not been altered by PuP Books. The phrases and usage reflect norms of the late twenties and early thirties and thus present an historical record of the time. In no way does PuP Books condone the use of similar phraseology in today's world.

In this fifth book of the Airplane Boys, Jim and Bob risk their lives to help a worthy family out of their difficulties.

CONTENTS

I

AN OLD ENEMY

"I say, Buddy, my esophagus feels as if my pharynx is severed," Robert Caldwell remarked very soberly to his step-brother, Jim Caldwell, as the pair made their way among the gay crowd attending the Spanish-Peruvian fiesta near Cuzco.

"That's right serious, old man. Think somebody shot an arrow into the air while you were asleep with your mouth open and it dropped in?" the older boy inquired with equal gravity.

"Is that any way to treat a fellow who is empty to his boot tips and just when I am beginning to discard vulgar slang for something real cultured in the way of language?" Bob demanded.

"Oh! Do you perchance happen to be trying to convey the idea that you are hungry? Why don't you say so in good old Texas, long may she reign, talk!"

"Well, when do we tank up?"

"Looks to me as if Carlos de Castro is going to be late. He said that he might, so we may as well make a landing and take on fuel," Jim agreed cheerfully. They proceeded toward the section where a number of tables were set up in stalls beside rows of tropical plants growing in tubs, but it appeared that Bob was not the only person who was anxious to get something to eat, for everyplace they saw was occupied.

"A table, Senors?" inquired a deferential waiter, who bowed with great politeness, then led the way to the further end of the serving space. He dragged a pair of kegs into the shelter of the foliage, swung a wide board over the top of them, produced a cloth from under his coat and with a great flourish smoothed it out. Two chairs appeared from behind a pile of boxes. "Presto," he smiled widely.

"Pronto," Bob replied. Placing one hand over his belt buckle, he bowed deeply. "Before me, esteemed brother."

"If I were behind you there is no telling what I'd do to you," Jim answered. "Why this reversion to days when knighthood was budding?" He took one of the seats and Caldwell the other.

"I'm letting Spanish manners get under my skin—"

"Looks more like wood-ticks—" Austin interrupted. "They make a horse skid around just that way."

"And I want to impress Mom when we get home, old man. Have you forgotten that we take the air at crack of dawn tomorrow and our bird is to set us down on the K-A ranch before the sun's evening rays can reach the peak of Cap Rock?"

"Sure I know." Jim's eyes glistened. "It'll be great to sail through space like that and so high that no one will see us, but just the same, me Flying Buddy, if you go acting like that around your mother, she'll think that something is the matter with you, and it will be a dose of oil for yours." At that the two laughed heartily, but their merriment was cut short by the appearance of the waiter with huge platters of mighty good-looking food, so they proceeded to do it justice.

"The meals in Peru are almost as good as in Texas," Bob remarked after he had helped himself and made his first attack.

"Right-O, but it will be grand to get home," Jim declared. They did not talk any more but gave their undivided attention to the meal, and while it was in process, they noted indifferently that two men had been ushered to the table the other side of the artificial hedge and a bit forward of their own. That place too had been put up roughly to accommodate the extra crowd and was a bit apart from the others. Jim, who was facing the festival, had the better view of the occupants and through the branches he could see the rather stout, stooped shoulders of one's back, and occasionally caught a glimpse of the other's face. He was a slender, dark man whose bearing was quite military, and about his lips played a smile that was more like a sneer than an indication of a cheerful disposition.

"Wall—I'm here," the heavier man announced with surliness, and Bob turned cautiously at the sound of that voice but couldn't see the faces of either men.

"So it is. You have a difficult time had," the first speaker began. "We will of refreshments partake, my good sir, then we can talk in this so exclusive little corner without fear—without undue fear," he added as he took the precaution to glance around. Jim bent his head low over his plate and it did not seem to occur to the man that another couple might have been placed so far beyond the dining space. "You had an accident and have been in the hospital."

"Yah. I sent you word from the hospital, didn't I?"

"That is true. It was grievous that your accident should have come at such an inopportune moment; when there was work for you," the other remarked, and there was an odd insinuation in his voice.

"If you, or your boss thinks I cracked up because I wanted to, you have got another think coming—see! I wasn't even piloting the plane when she came down—" There was anger in the tone and Jim saw the man's shoulders straighten and lean forward a trifle.

"Control your temper, my friend. I merely remarked it was too bad for you—"

"Oh, you did—well—maybe you got another guess coming on that too," the other answered. The waiter brought them wine, which they sipped in silence until the man was well out of ear-shot.

"Another guess, you say?"

"That's what I said." Bob, who had been leaning so that he could hear every word easily, glanced questioningly at Jim.

"Know them?" his lips formed, and Jim shook his head that he didn't.

"Do you?" he asked softly.

"One, I think. Listen!" They attended

to their own food as quietly as possible but every faculty was alert. Aside from noticing that the two men seemed an ill-assorted pair Jim had not been greatly interested, but now that Bob thought he recognized one of them, he was anxious to learn more. The Flying Buddies had managed to get into so many adventures since the summer months when they had dropped Her Highness down in Canada almost at the feet of a Royal Mounty and had offered to help the patrol man capture border-runners, that caution was a fixed habit with both of them. They had found that it paid.

"Now, look here," the stout man began aggressively, "I ain't a part of your outfit —see!"

"I observe, but you have worked—not too successfully—with us."

"Yah. I went into that fool Don business with Lilly Boome."

"Why broadcast?"

"Well, I did, and it wasn't my fault it didn't come out so good."

"That has been admitted by the chief himself. The Don is a very clever man."

"Yah, he is. I went there like I owned the place, and he put it all over us, like a crab-net, see? Now, I'm told you're wanting me to get work in this new power works down here—"

"It will not be difficult—"

"You haul in your horns. If it's so easy why don't you do it yourself? Now listen, I told you I don't belong to your outfit and I ain't taking orders from your chief—not me. See? I heard on good authority that there are some of the Don's own tribe in that works—and I'm not buttin' in against any of them. That's flat and final," he declared emphatically.

Then, into Jim's mind flashed the recollection of the evening he and Bob had dined with Don Haurea at the Box Z ranch, which adjoined the K-A along Cap Rock in Texas. They were so well entertained by their new friend that they failed to note the passage of the hours and it was quite late when an automobile brought a former housekeeper of the ranch, a lawyer with a brief-case full of legal documents, and a man whom they claimed was a son of Don Haurea's father. The Don had made short work of them, and now, Jim was sure that he recognized the broad back of Ollie, who had posed as the son. Even to the boys the scheme had seemed too stupid for anyone with a grain of sense to take part in or try to put over, but later the Don had explained that it was an attempt to get him and his property tied up by law. While there could be no possible doubt as to the outcome of the suit if the matter ever got as far as that, the rogues expected to have an uninterrupted opportunity to ferret out ancient secrets and perhaps find great wealth which they thought was concealed somewhere about the Box-Z Ranch. The Flying Buddies exchanged surprised glances, but neither moved nor spoke as they sat listening.

"You should not be afraid—" the man sneered.

"Afraid, that's good! Well, big boy, maybe I am afraid, but I'm not touchin' the job, see! I got something myself that ain't such little potatoes as blowing up a power plant or putting a crimp in the works. That's my answer."

"In your answer I am interested."

"Maybe you are, and maybe you ain't, but if you knew what it was, you would be—and how," Ollie retorted.

"You have perhaps discovered a gold mine!" the man suggested.

"I have, perhaps, and perhaps it's something better than gold. Now, you listen. You know I was flying with another guy to Cuzco to meet you, and we came down like a thousand bricks," Ollie said.

"That I have heard. I watched the funeral of the pilot and I sent to you flowers and jelly and wine to the hospital," the other man answered casually.

"Yah. Well, I crawled out of the wreck after somebody else had picked up the pilot and took him to the hospital. Then I tried to make a fire to keep warm by and signal, and while I was asleep it burned up what was left of the plane. I had to get a move on or be cooked myself, and I nearly was. I found some berries and roots that I ate and days afterward I managed to drag myself to a trapper's hut, and the man took me to the nearest settlement. Now—when I was crawling from that bon-fire, I found something swell—swell." He straightened his back and cocked back his head. "Waiter," he shouted. "More wine—plenty more."

"You should be moderate with wine after having been ill," the other man reminded him.

"Yah. Maybe I should. Not because I've been ill, but because I might talk too much—"

"You're not exactly tight-mouthed at the moment."

"Think you're funny, don't you? Well, you trot back to your High Chief, or whatever he is, and tell him if he's interested I'll go fifty-

fifty with him. He can divide his share anyway he likes, but fifty per cent is mine and no questions asked."

"Probably you have found an ancient Ynca treasure hole. They are being found every day, and when investigated—nothing more valuable than a crumbling mummy is revealed," the other told him.

"You ain't no good at guessin'. If I hadn't cracked the plane I'd go back and get the whole works myself, but you tell your chief that's my proposition," Ollie answered insolently. "A lot of guys will jump at the chance the minute I spring it, but you fellows get first crack."

"Very generous of you."

"Sure, I'm generous."

"Should I have the great audacity to return to my 'chief' as you call him, he would think me crazy, my friend. You'll have to give me something more than vague phrases to repeat to him. In the first place, your story is not convincing, regardless of what you found. You were injured, it was days before you reached the trapper's cabin, you could not return to the spot," the other objected.

"I ain't such a nut as I look. I can go right back to that spot, and don't you forget it," Ollie boasted.

"Did you make a map of the locality?"

"Ain't you cute? Why don't you ask if I have it with me?"

"You are too quick, my friend. It is unfair to be so sensitive. As a man of the world you are perfectly aware that no one would consider any proposition unless he knew what he is going after."

"All right, I'll tell you. It's platinum—" Ollie spoke more softly, but Bob understood what he said.

"My friend, there has been no platinum discovered in Peru in hundreds of years. There was, at one time, a small amount of it, but never a very great quantity. Not enough to make it worth thinking about. The world gets it in quantities from Russia, and these Andes have been searched diligently, but there is little here."

"That's where you are wrong."

"How do you know it was platinum?"

"Listen, big boy, during the war we had to have it, and I flew with some other lads into Russia to get it, see? We came out with it—I got more than any other man in the outfit, and I brought it back. I know what I'm talking about."

"That is indeed interesting. I shall present your proposition to the chief and I am sure that he will be most happy to discuss the matter with you." He extended his hand with a smile and Ollie accepted it with a swaggering toss of his head.

"I knew I'd get you on the run. Come on, I want to have a dance with one of those Spanish girls—they sure have pretty girls here." The pair rose quickly and a moment later strode off toward the dancing pavilion.

"Whew! Wouldn't that rattle your great-aunt's false teeth!" Bob whistled.

"Or make the dear lady do a Highland Fling," Jim added. "So, this is where little Ollie took himself after he left the Don's that night. Guess the United States got kind of hot for him. Wonder if he has discovered platinum?"

"Well, if he has, he'll never see a flake of it," Bob remarked soberly. "That Chief, or whatever he is, will get the whole shooting match away from him so quickly it'll make his head spin."

"Let's have some dessert and if Carlos doesn't show up by the time we've finished, we'd better go home. The mail will be in and there will be letters from Dad and your mother."

"Suits me," Bob agreed. They motioned to the waiter and ordered a pastry, but before it was half finished, Jim happened to look up.

"Here comes Carlos now. Somebody is

with him." Bob glanced around and then they saw that a man was following Carlos, or rather walking close behind him.

"Senors, I have searched for you," Carlos called, then he stopped as the man came closer.

"Pardon, senor. You picked up a wallet which was dropped by my friend who was taken ill," he said very politely.

"Yes, I did pick up some sort of case, but I don't know about handing it over to a stranger," Carlos answered good-naturedly.

"My friend was taken ill and is now on the way to the hospital," the man urged. "I am distressed and would go to him at once."

"Yes, of course," the young fellow hesitated, then the man stepped close and one hand was pressed against Carlos' side. The Flying Buddies saw the move, and sprang up.

"I say, old thing, what's the idea?" Bob demanded.

"Sure you are not off your wave length?" Jim added. Four fists were clenched hard and two pairs of eyes flashed angrily. "Keep your hand in your pocket, old timer." They shoved in between their pal and the chap who accosted him, but just as they did so, two huge men leaped from the background and one of them caught Carlos on the chin with such a crack that he dropped to the floor, but he rolled over on his face before the fellow could put a hand into his breast pocket. In a moment fists and feet were flying in a grand free-for-all, and someone, probably the manager of the place, pranced about trying to round up the fighters into a shed or anyplace out of sight of the crowd.

"My business, my business," he wailed, then, almost as suddenly as the scrap had started, the three boys were yanked to their feet and they found themselves in a huge kitchen.

"He stole a wallet that belongs to my friend," the first chap accused. "Search him and you'll find it." A very tall man in a clean white suit stepped forward as if to carry out the request, but Jim quickly put a detaining hand on the fellow's arm.

"I say, listen—" he urged. The man looked down at the boy and for the briefest instant his eyes rested on the green emerald ring he always wore. "That chap is lying—"

"Put them out," he snapped to a huge attendant, who looked more like a great gorilla than a human being.

"Si."

"I tell you—"

"Depart." In less time than it takes to tell it, the assaulting party were kicked out of the kitchen, down a pair of slippery stairs and into a shallow hole used for slop water. They cursed and sputtered alternately, but the bouncer raised his foot again, so they scrambled away from the vicinity as fast as they could go.

"Your names, young gentlemen," the tall chap said politely.

"I'm Jim Austin," the Flying Buddy began and proceeded to introduce his companions.

"And I am Alonzo de Zimmon. I regret that you should have had such an unpleasant experience in my establishment." He held out his hand to Bob, who promptly accepted it, and his eyes rested on the mate to Caldwell's ring. "It has given me great pleasure to meet you young Americans. And you, also, Senor de Castro. Your father I know well."

"Of course, I've heard him speak of you, Don de Zimmon. We certainly are obligated to you for helping us," Carlos replied. "My father will come and thank you just as soon as I tell him how greatly we are indebted to you."

"It will give me great pleasure to take you home in my car," the Don answered. "I am about to drive your way."

"Thanks a lot," Jim accepted.

"We do not wish to inconvenience you, sir," Carlos said quickly.

"Not at all," answered the Don, then added, "Unless you desire to remain longer at the festival."

"Reckon we're willing to call it a day," said Bob ruefully looking at their clothes, which were rumpled and dusty.

"Even so, you are not so disheveled and unpresentable as your late opponents," the Don smiled.

II

DELAYED RETURN

When Don de Zimmon's limousine drew up before the palatial home of the de Castros, there was real concern on the face of Pedro de Castro as he came to greet them.

"My old friend, Alonzo, it is indeed a great pleasure to see you but your looks are all so grave that I am anxious to know if trouble has befallen any of you."

"A little scrap, Padre, that's all. We were so mussed, that is, our clothes, that Senor de Zimmon generously gave us a lift, which we accepted instead of waiting for the car." Carlos spoke lightly.

"Your son, my friend, is not unlike we were, you and I, in long past days when adventure made our blood hot, but although we thought nothing of facing danger, we carefully concealed details from families if we were able. He is only partly correct in his statement. It was because I felt that something more serious might occur that I urged an immediate return home. I should have been most distressed had I permitted them to come unattended," the Don replied.

"Many exploits we shared, my old friend, but it was always you who faced the greatest danger and whose deeds were most daring. On your heels I was a courageous fellow—ready to attack a lion—but alone—" he shrugged his shoulders, "alone I was given to going the long way around."

"You do not do yourself justice. Once I recall that your sword saved me when my own had been broken; and another time you fought off a hungry shark—"

"It was nothing—" old Pedro said quickly.

"Nothing, Padre? You never told me anything about those times!"

"Perhaps some day we will talk of them. Tell me this moment, what danger threatened these sons of my friends in the United States, and my own boy?"

"They were attacked at the fiesta by a lot of ruffians and came rolling into the kitchen of the Santa Maria just as I entered to speak to my manager. My first impulse was to have them kicked out." As he spoke his eyes rested a moment on Jim, then he proceeded, "but I saw that they were not all of the same breed, so I had the scum booted and brought these boys home to you because

I feel sure that the men who assaulted them would not be satisfied with the outcome of the combat."

"That is indeed serious. Let us go to the portico where it is cool, and let me hear at once the facts. I beg of you, my dear Don, come with us, then I shall surely get the full particulars from these young people." The three boys glanced at each other ruefully, but they followed the old gentlemen and were soon seated about a small table in the shade of great palm trees close by the pool with its tall fountain from which the water shot high, then dropped back on the glistening foliage. A servant brought iced drinks, and when they were comfortably settled, the host's eyes sought his son's with a question.

"I don't understand it, Padre, I'd promised the Buddies that I would join them at the fiesta the minute I could get there, and I was much later than I expected to be. To save time, I hired a cab and had the man drive me around the further side because I thought I could reach the boys more directly. I paid the man and he went off, then I noticed another car coming along the road. There wasn't anything special about that, only it seemed strange anyone should come to the festival by that route, but I dismissed the matter because I'd come by that route myself."

"Yes?"

"The car was being driven very slowly as if the chauffeur expected to pick up someone he had not located. Then, as I hurried along, I saw two men coming rather quickly, supporting a third man between them. His feet rather dragged but not as if he was drunk and his hands, or one of them, was fumbling in the front of his coat. His hat was on the back of his head, which was moving from side to side, and just as they drew close, it was knocked off. One of the men bent and picked it up and then I caught a glance of the sick man's face. It was very flushed, but his eyes looked as if he was perfectly aware of what was taking place. They put his hat on, the chauffeur blew his horn softly, and in a moment the three got into the car and it was driven away quickly."

"Extraordinary!"

"I didn't think much about that at the moment, then it dawned upon me that the man's eyes were more fearful than ill. I paused at the spot where his hat dropped wondering if I should report the matter, then, right at my feet I saw a wallet. I supposed it belonged to the third man, so I picked it up, determined to hand it over to the police as soon as possible. Then I hurried to join our friends, and had just succeeded in finding their table and calling a greeting when a stranger touched my arm from behind and begged that I return the wallet which he was going to take to his sick friend."

"That's when we saw him," Jim put in.

"Ordinarily I should have done so without a question, for the chap was gentlemanly enough, but the look in that man's eyes sort of got me, so I told him I was not sure that I should. Immediately his face got ugly and he poked his fingers into my ribs and demanded that I hand it over at once and from right behind him jumped two huge fellows. One of them landed his fist on my jaw, then I believe the Flying Buddies came on with their engines wide open. I felt one of the men make a dive to my pocket, so I managed to roll over and keep my coat closed tightly. After that I felt as if I'd landed in a hive of mad bees and I couldn't get up until the chief dragged me to my feet. One of the men accused me of stealing the wallet and demanded that I be searched, but the Don stepped in and took command. That's all I know."

"What sort of looking men were they, my son?"

"The two who supported him were tall, well-built fellows. The sick man was quite stout and wore a dark suit. I should say that he was an American; he was quite fair."

Although this description was not very complete, the Flying Buddies exchanged glances.

"Wonder if it was Ollie?" Bob ventured.

"And who is this Ollie?" the Don asked with interest.

"He's—I don't know much about what he is, really, but we saw him the first time in Don Haurea's home a year ago, and today he was at the table nearest to ours on the other side of the hedge," Bob replied, then proceeded with an account of the affair to which the gentlemen listened attentively.

"And you are guessing that this so-called sick man may be this one to whom you listened?"

"It popped into my head, sir. I just thought that if his companion at the table wanted to get information from him, he might have arranged to take him off the grounds in some way," Bob answered.

"They must have worked fast," Jim added.

"Those fellows aren't exactly slow motion movers," said Bob.

"No, they are not."

"Have you heard anything of recent platinum discoveries?" the Don inquired.

"No, I have not, but according to this 'Ollie's' statement, he had kept the secret to himself," Pedro de Castro reminded them.

"We all know that the Andes are rich with treasure of one sort or another and many expeditions have been financed to search for the precious metal, but I understand that our geologists agree that while there may be small quantities of it in different sections it is of a poor quality and in places where getting it out would cost more than it is worth," the Don told them.

"That is quite true. I have seen the report. When the Spaniards came to this land there was a good deal, or rather the Indians had quantities of it; they called it 'frog gold' but at that time the white men knew nothing of its value and would not have it. Later a great deal was accumulated and shipped to Spain, then the supply diminished until now it is almost gone. Now it is Russia that is rich with the mineral," Senor de Castro explained.

"Well, I say, Carlos, we can soon settle if the chap was Ollie. Perhaps the name is on his wallet," Jim suggested.

"I never thought of that." Carlos grinned and produced it from his inside pocket. He handed it to his father and the older man turned it over carefully. It was as long as a legal-sized envelope, made of very soft thin Russian leather, with three long folds. When it was opened wide they saw two small flaps in the middle to be brought down over the ends of bills or papers, while the outside edges were stitched to form a pocket. Senor de Castro examined it carefully but there wasn't a scrap of paper of any description in it.

"Empty as a last year's bird's nest," Jim remarked.

"Quite empty," their host replied.

"It's a nice looking wallet, but shivering sharks, what is there about that to fight over?" Bob exploded.

"It is very mysterious," Senor de Castro responded soberly. He handed it to his friend, who also scrutinized it thoroughly.

"Not so much as an initial scratched on it," he declared.

"Some mystery," Jim put in. "Perhaps Carlos was seen picking the wallet up and they were not taking any chances on losing the secret."

"Yes," Bob added, "We don't know that it is Ollie's."

"That is true. We do not. In fact, we know little more than we did before we examined it. I should suggest that you retain possession of it for the present and I can make judicious inquiries as to the identity of the owner. If he were really ill, it is more than likely that he is now in the hospital, and he could not be admitted without a name. It was strange indeed that a gang of ruffians should make such an effort to secure it, unless they did not know how barren it was. Now, my good friend, I think it would be well for our young people to—as it is so aptly put in America, scrutinize their step."

"We'll watch our step, and our hop too," Jim laughed.

"Yes. We are off for home in the morning so I guess there are no more Peruvian adventures for us," Bob grinned cheerfully.

"Then, I shall tell you it is with regret that I bid you good evening, and I trust that I shall have the pleasure of meeting you again." The Don extended his hand cordially, and both boys rather wished that they had had a chance to know him better.

"If you ever get to the bottom of this puzzle I hope you will let us know, sir."

"I shall be delighted." The Don took his departure, and when Senor de Castro returned to the portico the boys were still puzzling over the empty wallet.

"You will be careful," he urged.

"Of course. Don de Zimmon seems like a

mighty fine man. You must have had some wonderful times when you were growing up," Bob remarked.

"We had some wonderful times, but we did not grow up together. The Don is Peruvian, although he speaks little of his forefathers. He came here with his family when he was a lad in his teens and we attended the same school; also we went off to college and after that we drifted apart. The Don traveled extensively in the Orient, and a few years ago he returned to Cuzco with his wife and children. They are a fine family, splendid citizens," Senor de Castro explained.

"Tell us about that shark business, Padre," Carlos insisted.

"You have forgotten that your suits need to be changed," his father reminded him.

"That's so," they had to admit, so they could not press the man for the story, although it sounded mighty thrilling. When they returned, ready for dinner, a cable was handed to Jim, who opened and decoded it quickly.

> "We miss you much, but I wish that you would stay until the analysis is made and bring the report with you. I shall feel safer than trusting it to the regular carriers. All well here. Dad."

"It will give us pleasure to have you remain," Carlos chuckled when the message was read to him and his father.

"It will take perhaps two days to get the report and I believe that Senor Austin's caution is very wise," the older man declared. Although the Flying Buddies were anxious to get home and the message gave them a deep feeling of disappointment, they kept it to themselves, and grinned as if delighted at the postponement.

"Doubtless you will learn more of the mystery of my sick friend, or your Ollie," Carlos suggested.

"It'll be great to know what the answer is," Jim responded cheerfully.

Later that evening when they were in Jim's room, Caldwell lingered at the door. "I say, we were lucky that Don de Zimmon could tell us from the roughnecks." Austin looked at him a moment.

"It was lucky that we were wearing the green emerald rings that Yncicea Haurea gave us that day we rescued him off the Island in Lake Champlain," he replied softly.

"The rings?" Bob glanced at his.

"Sure. The Don saw mine first then had a look at yours when he shook hands with you. Guess he's one of the Ynca descendants."

"I might have known he couldn't pick us out of that mess. Gee, Buddy, what a lot of things we have nose-dived into since the boy gave us those rings. I am rather glad we are staying over, perhaps we'll see the Don again and I'd like to know if that sick lad was Ollie."

"Me too. Suppose we better get to bed now, I'm tired as the very dickens," Jim remarked.

"So am I, in a way, but I'm kind of hankerin' to have a look at the 'Lark'—"

"You mean that you want to go joy riding along the milky way," Jim grinned. "Well, reckon I'm not too tired for that, but we don't want to overdo it—just a little hop or the De Castros will be worried stiff."

"Just a little one," Bob nodded eagerly. They did not wait to do more than slip into light jackets, then they went quietly out of the house and made their way unnoticed to the new hangar where they found the "Lark" resting as if poised for immediate flight into the starry heavens. She was a beautifully built plane with all known, and several as-yet-unknown, modern improvements, for it was a gift from Don Haurea in grateful acknowledgement of services rendered him and his immediate family by the Flying Buddies. Their first plane had proudly borne the name of Her Highness, but some enemy bent on revenge had ruined her, and had almost killed Bob too.

"She does look good. Let's not light up this place; it may attract attention from the house and Senor de Castro will think something is wrong," Jim proposed, as he opened the door to the cock-pit.

"Suits me." Bob climbed into the pilot seat and while he adjusted the parachute, Austin glanced at the radio instrument then suddenly switched off the light on the control board.

"What's up—"

"I don't know. Look at the dials," Jim whispered, and then Bob noticed an odd green light playing about the rims of the instrument.

"It's the signal from the Laboratory," Bob said softly.

"Green means anger. Some one who is hopping mad is around here, Buddy. Scrutinize your process, old timer."

"Perhaps you'd better see how things are in the back," Caldwell said aloud, quite as if they had no warning of danger.

"All right, but why the heck didn't you look before you climbed in?" Jim grumbled. Instead of jumping out of the cock-pit in the normal fashion, he leaped over the back, stepped onto the fuselage, then swung onto the wing. In a moment he had pushed a button and immediately the place was a blaze of light.

"Well, look who's here," Bob exclaimed in astonishment, and Jim dropped on his stomach to look over the side.

"If it ain't the Dolly Sisters," he grinned.

"Blast you—" The explosion came from the contorted lips of the huge man, one who had tried to get the wallet from Carlos' pocket earlier that day. Beside him, crouched to spring, and with a heavy monkey wrench ready to bring down on some defenseless head, was the other big fellow.

"We nearly had a couple of stowaways," Bob said cheerfully.

"Wonder if their little playmate is hanging around. Guess I'll ring the alarm bell at the house." Jim proceeded to carry out the plan and in a moment they heard a bell ringing in the distance and immediately the windows of the great house leaped to life as lights flooded through the darkness. They heard a sound as of a heavy body jumping off of one of the upper verandas, then the swift scramble of racing feet. Shouts came from every direction, and the two men in the garage seemed to be making a terrific effort to get away, but they could barely move.

"Bet it's the first time they touched a live wire," Bob remarked, but just then the power was turned off, and with a series of furious curses, the two ruffians dashed out of the place as fast as their legs could carry them.

"The Lab men caught them good and proper," Jim remarked with satisfaction. "Reckon they were released to avoid explanations. We can fix that up, all right."

"Boy, Jim—Bob—"

"O.K., sir, here," Jim shouted.

"Are you safe, are you injured—oh—"

"We're great," Jim answered quickly. "We thought we'd like a little ride before we turned in, but we found two fellows out here, so we rang the house bell to scare them off—"

"Oh, it is fortunate you did," Carlos said quickly as he came puffing up in his pajamas. "The bell rang, woke me up, and there was a man in my room, just going through my pockets. He jumped so fast I could not be positive, but I believe it was the man who asked me for the wallet this afternoon." Just then they heard a series of loud shots, and running out, were in time to see a man servant, gun smoking in his hand, bring down a chap as he leaped a high fence. The man fell and they ran to the spot. The fellow was dead. There was no mistaking that face, and the boys turned away a bit sick at the sight of the bleeding body.

"I got one, sir—" Another servant dragged the man who had jumped from the veranda.

"Lock him securely until morning," Senor de Castro ordered.

"All for an empty purse," Carlos remarked.

"Hey—" There came another shout and a moment later two more men were captured. One had fallen and injured his leg, but the other was unhurt.

"Look after them. Why are you men turning into such devils?"

"To get something you don't know anything about. That wallet you've been trying to kill me for is empty—there isn't a scrap in it," Carlos told them. Those who could, looked at him sullenly, but the one who was hurt snarled furiously,

"Maybe it is empty," he rasped, "and then again, maybe it ain't, see!"

III

UNIDENTIFIED

"Morning, Buddy. What do you suppose that guy meant last night when he said, 'maybe there wasn't and maybe there was' something in that wallet? It got my ailerons flapping," Bob said as he came into Jim's room. His Flying Buddy was already half dressed, although no one in the De Castro household was astir at that hour.

"That got my think tank clanking, too, but I reckon the old bean's crusted, for I can't make it out. I reached a lot of conclusions, you can take your choice. Perhaps he was just shooting off his mouth; he may think the wallet Carlos picked up is something different from what it is, and then again, it's possible that there is something about the leather case which contains the secret. We couldn't find anything more when we looked at it last night before it was locked in the safe after they tried to steal it," Austin answered.

"You haven't anything on me as a deductor. Now, all we have to do is eliminate all but one, and there we are with the answer," Bob grinned.

"Right-O. Any ideas on which to eliminate?"

"My dear step-brother, companion of my youth, I can argue with fervor for each and every one of them, or, with equal conviction against them."

"We're equally dumb. Let's form a trust. Sure you didn't forget to tell Senor de Castro that we were going up for a bracer this morning? We don't want him to think that some doo-doo kidnaped us."

"I told him. Said that we'd be here in time for breakfast, so let's get a move on. Ah, 'Lark,' I hear you calling me!"

A bit later the Flying Buddies were again in the hangar beside the graceful little plane. This time they took the precaution of having a good look about the place to make sure that no one was hanging around ready to throw a monkey wrench at their heads, or concealed in the "Lark" itself. On the trip from the United States they had found a stowaway while flying above the Caribbean Sea and the vicious brute had fought savagely to bring them down. A few days after their arrival, enemies of Mr. Austin had secreted a huge poisonous snake in the communication tube between the two cock-pits. It had crawled leisurely out over the nearly paralyzed Bob who was taking pictures of the coast from the back. With the settlement of the Power-Plant difficulties and the apprehension of the ring-leaders, the boys had felt safe from further attempts, but it was now evident that their association with Carlos de Castro had started a new string of enemies on their trail. Although the men had been captured the night before, there were probably others on the outside who would seek revenge because of the failure of the attack, or make further efforts to get possession of the mysterious wallet.

"All's well that ends well," Bob called when his share of the inspection was finished.

"Here too. Hop in," Jim urged. Presently they were both ready and Austin took the controls, the engine started a cheering roar, the propeller whirled, and the plane rolled lightly along the run-way, curved a bit, her nose lifted and she began to climb eagerly into the air. The Flying Buddies grinned at each other and their eyes glistened happily.

"This is the life," Bob bellowed, and Jim nodded. It was a clear, beautiful morning. The sky in the east was tinted with long pinkish grey streaks which announced the coming of the sun from beneath the horizon. They had made no plan as to where they would go, but just started with the unconquerable desire to fly, and as the plane scrambled into the heavens they filled their lungs with deep breaths of pure joy. Up and up they raced until the altitude meter read three thousand feet, then the pilot leveled off, made a wide circle, and flipped her into a double loop just to relieve their feelings. He pulled her out with nicety, then leveled off and shot forward.

"Let's go over Amy-Ran," Bob proposed.

"Right-O."

The course was quickly calculated and the plane's nose pointed in the direction of the ancient fastness which was still the property of the descendants of the famous Yncas, whose people had once inhabited the vast empire which was the world's most civilized and prosperous government. Jim increased the speed and the plane roared through the sky above the magnificent Andes Mountains with their numberless spurs and beautiful valleys, which looked as if only the greatest of nature's artists had been entrusted to shape their perfect outline. Here and there were high plains whose smooth surfaces looked as if they were set with glistening opals, while others were dark-wooded with forests which were broken only by lovely lakes of crystal-clear water that reflected the sky above them like wonderful mirrors. The sun, rising with a splendid burst of brilliance, sent its rays flashing until every inch they touched leaped to life and color.

The Flying Buddies took in all of the marvelous scenes rolling beneath them, and were intensely sorry for grounded chaps who had never experienced the thrill of viewing such a panorama to the accompaniment of wind singing through the wires of an airplane carrying them swiftly through space between the earth and sky. Finally, in the distance, they made out the S-shaped plateau of Amy-Ran, whose edge was rimmed like a crown with the giant stone that had once formed a section of its inaccessible fortress.

In a few minutes the "Lark" was circling like a bird above one end and as Jim calculated his landing he recalled the day Carlos de Castro had brought them to the spot, the day that young Arthur Gordon had so mysteriously appeared and assaulted them. There had been no means of escape from the precipitous rock or the murderous attack of the Texas outlaw and Austin had been sure that it was only a matter of minutes before their three lifeless bodies would be pounced upon by hungry vultures whose nests were secreted on nearby crags. When his Buddies lay helpless, Jim was standing before a black-nosed revolver but before its trigger could be pressed Yncicea Haurea and his uncle Corso stepped into the ruin and the tide of battle was swiftly and effectively turned. The motor was silenced and the "Lark" was gliding quietly down.

"I'm taking her where she can be a bit out of sight."

"Great brain work. Never know who may take the air with a view to doing scout work. Peaceful spot, this old Peru, when there is no one about," said Bob. He too had been thinking of the wild experiences they had been through, but his thoughts had been on the more recent happenings, and as they made the descent his eyes lingered with amusement at the nearby peak which a few nights before had given a perfect imitation of a seething volcano with tons of burning lava rushing threateningly on Gordon and his gang. If it had been the real thing, the Flying Buddies and the two De Castros would have been buried under many feet of molten rock and cinders. But as a piece of clever stage business it had struck terror into the hearts of the man with the green mask and his companions. In their mad rush to get above the danger zone several of them had been killed.

"Give a calf enough rope and he'll hang himself," Caldwell remarked as the plane's wheels touched the chosen landing spot and rolled a few feet. "Queer how many of those guys have eliminated themselves in one way or another."

"Yes. I should think they'd begin to tumble to themselves that they are amateurs and quit trying to get the better of the men they are so intent on robbing," Jim answered. The plane rolled beneath the shelter of the fortress wall and when she was in a position where she could not be seen by curious flyers, he brought her to a stop. "I have a hunch that some bright lad in that gang may come flying about to have a look at the remains of the volcano."

"Well, won't he get the jolt of his gay careless youth when he can't find a crater as big as a hole in a tooth?" chuckled Bob. "Any hunches that we'll find a Lab. man around?"

"Thought we might," Jim admitted.

"And presto, I appear!" It was Ynilea, who smiled broadly. "I too am becoming subject to attacks of hunch and when we found that you were not going to go home this morning under central power I observed your hilarious flight and was delighted when you determined to pay Amy-Ran another visit."

"Gee, did you see the party they tried to pull last night?" Bob demanded quickly.

"Not the 'party' but the records this morning."

"A man called Ollie had a plane smash-up somewhere in the Andes and thinks he discovered a rich deposit of platinum," Jim explained.

"Where?" Ynilea was interested.

"I don't know," the boy answered, then went on and told of the conversation they had overheard in the Santa Maria and the later attack of the chap who wanted the wallet.

"We don't know yet if it is the same man but it looks as if it might be," Bob put in. "I say—" He stopped abruptly, for their quick ears had caught the unmistakable hum of an airplane motor, "that one of your crates?"

"No." Ynilea listened intently. "No."

They sat very still as the sound grew in volume, then the Lab. man stepped cautiously toward the place where the boys had run the "Lark" under cover. Quickly the Flying Buddies jumped out of straps and parachutes and hurried after him. In a moment they were making their way along the outer edge of the great wall, much as Carlos had said he did when he came there as a small boy and thought he saw an opening into a court. They proceeded carefully, keeping out of sight of the approaching airman, until suddenly Ynilea held up his hand. Just ahead of them they saw the Indian woman whose age no one could ever guess, coming very slowly from the opposite direction. She was wearing a robe which hung in folds from her shoulders, a loose hood covered her head, and the material looked so exactly like the stones beside which she walked that if she had not moved she could not have been distinguished from one of them. She seemed to be aware of their presence, for in a moment she stopped, made a slight movement of her head, and Ynilea instantly went to her, the boys close at his heels.

"Come," she said softly.

Her hand, still concealed by the folds of her sleeve, moved over the nearest stone, and after an instant, during which the Flying Buddies almost held their breaths, the great mass moved. It slipped back about three inches, then slid along like a folding door, leaving an opening wide enough for them all to enter. The boys drew quick breaths of astonishment as they found themselves in a good-sized room which was cut out of the solid rock of the mountain. The heavy panel returned to its place, and a moment later they stood close together on another rock which dropped with perfect smoothness about ten feet, then admitted them into another small room. This seemed to be in the section near the edge of the cliff. Ynilea moved back a part in one corner, and through a clever screen of foliage they could get a good view of the sky.

"My gosh, Carlos was right, he did see an opening in the wall," Bob said softly, and Ynilea turned a questioning glance toward him.

"He and some boys were here, I mean on top, years ago, and the little fellow declared he saw an opening in the wall. He was separated from his fellows, but when he found them and wanted to show it to them, he couldn't locate it again and they thought he was dreaming, or his imagination working over-time," Jim explained.

"His story was not credited?" Ynilea was adjusting a sort of periscope.

"No. He was such a little fellow they were sure he was mistaken."

"Oh, there she is," the tall Indian announced. He turned a wheel in the instrument and the boys could easily see the plane they had heard circling in a wide loop over their heads. As they watched, the man adjusted the glass until it was like a powerful telescope and Jim whistled as the flying machine was brought close enough for them to see the dark face of the pilot who was leaning over the side of his plane. He seemed to be looking for something and scowled when he did not find it.

"Bet the first gold tooth I get against a plugged dime that your hunch was right, Buddy. He is looking for the crater and the evidence of the near-disaster."

"He's coming lower." The plane, which had been almost at the ceiling, began to spiral, and the man in the cock-pit pressed a pair of field glasses to his eyes.

"He might pick us out—"

"The glass is not directed this way. As you say, he is looking for that crater," Ynilea answered.

"Be a nice little treat if you could really shoot off a lid and chase him with a blast of smoke and fire," Jim chuckled.

"It would indeed," Ynilea agreed with a smile.

"Give him something to write home about."

"Looks as if he is planning to land," Jim explained, and the plane was descending closer. Soon it was so near that the pilot did not require the glasses, and again he stared with a puzzled scowl toward the cliff which was supposed to have erupted. Then his machine began to rock crazily and bump as if it were riding deep, choppy waves, and for the next few minutes he had to give his undivided attention to maintaining his equilibrium. As he attended strictly to his job they could no longer see him, but they could see that he had struck something which threatened to end his flight in a wreck. He banked, curved, climbed, and dived in a desperate effort to force himself out of the pocket, or whatever it was that he had struck, but it wasn't until he was almost a speck in the sky again that he really recovered his balance. A moment later, the glass was pressed to his eyes and he stared through space as if determined to solve the mystery. Twice he descended quickly, but each time the plane misbehaved, so at last he gave it up, circled once more, then leveled off and shot away in the direction from which he had come.

"Pleasant entertainment while it lasted," laughed Bob. "Thought for a while we'd have him on our piazza."

"Sorry he didn't stick long enough to give you a really good time," laughed Ynilea. "One reason I wanted to see you boys today is to tell you that we have a small television we'll attach to the 'Lark's' radio. We were going to wait until you landed back in Texas to have it installed, but since you are staying over, we'll fix it in a set and exchange it for you as soon as it's ready. You can pay a visit to the Lab. to learn how it works."

"Oh, that will be great. I say, you'll soon have that plane so we won't need to come to the ground at all," announced Bob.

"Should you like that?"

"And how! But, Buddy we'd better get home or the De Castros will think we're lost—or never coming down," Jim warned.

"Too true," agreed Bob.

Presently the "Lark" was again in the air, but no "pockets or bumps" interfered with her flight when she leveled off, her nose pointed toward the De Castro home, and she rushed swiftly to the music of singing engine and whistling wind. The boys were perfectly satisfied with their morning adventure, but when they lighted on the runway, they saw Carlos waiting for them on the piazza.

"My father was getting distressed," he told them soberly.

"Sorry we over-stayed," Jim apologized.

"You are not so very much behind time, but there is some surprising news. Will you join us as you are? It's quite all right if you care to do so."

"We'll get there more quickly," Bob answered, so they hurried to the cool breakfast room off the portico, where they found Senor de Castro pacing the floor.

"I beg your pardon, sir—" Jim began.

"That's all right, my boy, breakfast is a movable feast. Did my son tell you the news?"

"No sir."

"Well, the man you call Ollie was found late last night. He had been beaten and his skull crushed to a pulp. He is dead."

"As Hamlet's cat," Carlos added, glancing at Bob. "Padre is a bit anxious about you—and me too—and he wants us to be mighty careful."

"We will, senor," Jim assured him.

"It seems that the police have traced the man's movements, questioned persons who saw him, including the attendants at the fiesta. No one seems to know who was with him when he had refreshments. As I remember that was when you boys overheard his conversation about the platinum."

"That's right," answered Jim.

"In such a case suspicious characters are rounded up and held until their innocence is established. They have several of these men and ask you to come to the detention quarters and see if you can identify any of them."

"Have you any idea when they picked up those men?" Jim inquired.

"Very early this morning."

"Then they have the wrong fellows."

"How do you know?"

"Because I saw the man in an airplane this morning. He was flying very much higher than we were, and looking over the side. I saw him quite plainly, sir."

"Was that the lad?" demanded Bob.

"I'm sure of it," Jim nodded.

"Could you describe the plane?" Carlos wanted to know.

"I could do that," Jim answered, then he frowned thoughtfully. "If he's a member of the gang we've been having all the fire-works with he or some of his gang may try to waylay us on the way home. Could the information be given to the police confidentially?"

"That shall be attended to, my boy. You early birds do manage to—"

"Gobble the worms," Bob suggested.

IV

A DISTRESS CALL

Immediately after breakfast the Sky Buddies, Carlos and Senor de Castro went to the office of the Detention Bureau where, without being observed themselves, they took a good look at several men held under suspicion as implicated in the murder of Ollie Boome. Although the three boys were mighty careful in the scrutinizing they agreed they had never seen any of the prisoners before. Then Jim wrote a detailed description of the airplane they had seen hovering over Amy-Ran fortress, also as good an account as possible of the pilot, for police broadcasting through North and South America. Where and how this information was obtained was to be kept a strict secret. That was arranged by Senor de Castro without difficulty.

"Any time you young travelers desire to pay us a visit and go through the prisons, we shall be most delighted to have the pleasure of escorting you," the official promised elaborately. The Flying Buddies had caught glimpses of the pens, cells, yards, high wall and guards which were sufficient to satisfy their natural curiosity.

"Thank you very much," Jim said politely.

"Next time we come to Peru we'll not forget," Bob added. He was thinking at the moment that if men and boys could get a peek at the place they would turn their talents toward something which would keep them out of jails. It seemed strange that anyone should risk freedom, liberty and the respect of his fellows by breaking laws which were made for the general good of all in order to get possession of something which did not belong to him. They were very thoughtful as they drove home and when the Flying Buddies stood on the broad piazza overlooking the beautiful land, Jim drew a deep breath.

"Tough luck, isn't it?"

"What."

"Those fellows held in there until we could come and look them over. Imagine being on that platform, made to stand up, turn around, put their heads up and down, show their hands and walk before a thick curtain. Of course they knew that someone, or maybe a dozen people were back of it examining them as if they were bugs under a glass, and whoever those people were would recognize them again no matter where they saw them, and know that they were men branded by the police."

"I was thinking of things like that too," Bob nodded soberly.

"Probably they will be let go, but they must have some sort of bad record, or they wouldn't be rounded up like that, and I suppose whenever a crime is committed, they stand the chance of being hauled in again.

"Uneasy lies the head—"

"Go on, you're mind's wandering. Their heads do not wear crowns," Jim interrupted.

"I was going to wax into poetry myself and say, uneasy lies the head that gets a man into difficulties, but it doesn't sound so good at that," answered Bob ruefully. "Here's the mail and a package." They accepted several items from the servant who had just appeared. One was a message from the Central Laboratory saying that some agricultural experiments were ready if Caldwell was interested. If the Flying Buddies would bring the "Lark" to Amy-Ran Fastness the new radio could be installed while the development was under observation. The package was from Don Haurea himself and contained some electrical and chemical instruments and compounds for Jim's special attention, for Austin was taking a very advanced course from the Laboratory in Texas. During their absence from home he had continued his studies, and since the return was delayed for a while, Don Haurea had some of his scientific men forward things which could be tried out without elaborate equipment.

"I say, old man, look." Bob held out his message eagerly, for making things grow and improving the land on the ranches in Texas was his chief ambition. "Come along—"

"Wait a minute. I've got something I can work on here. Suppose you take the plane and look after the onions, or whatever it is. I'll stay and see if I can get any results with this. You don't mind flying alone, do you? They'll keep their eyes on the "Lark." The radio-television can be installed and when you get home you can show me the works."

"Suits me, but Jim, bet you are going to miss something great—why, you know farmers—"

"Sure I do. They have no idea how much more they could do with their land. I know your whole spiel, old hayseed," Jim laughed.

"If it wasn't for the farmers you wouldn't

get anything to eat," Bob retorted good-naturedly.

"That's why I like them so well. Fly away, little boy, fly away," Jim urged, and a few minutes later he was in his own room, his coat off and an array of books opened before him.

Carefully he removed the apparatus and set to work. He glanced up as the plane thundered into the sky, and although he would have enjoyed going along, he was even more familiar with the great Laboratory and its workers than Bob was, so he did not mind remaining behind. He was so absorbed in what he was doing that the hours slipped by and it wasn't until a servant brought in an attractive looking lunch tray that he remembered the two De Castros had said they would not be home for the mid-day meal. They had made the trip to the power-plant in the huge limousine because it would be most convenient that day, and their own private plane was left in the hangar, which was built to accommodate three machines. Of course the plane was not so well equipped as the "Lark," but she was the last word in flying machines as modern inventors could make them. The night of the "stage volcano" the family's first plane had been stolen, but it had proved so useful that Senor de Castro immediately purchased another. This one he kept under guard both at home and at the works so that her instruments could not be tampered with and her fliers could not get into such dangerous situations as that stormy night when the compass had played them false because the needle hand had been deflected. For no reason at all those things slipped through Jim's mind as he ate his solitary lunch, but when it was finished he turned his attention to the task at hand, and everything else was dismissed.

"Senor, please—" Jim looked up and saw the servant, his face deeply anxious and through his mind flashed an idea that something had happened to Bob.

"What is it?" he demanded quickly. Glancing at his watch he noticed that it was nearly the middle of the afternoon.

"A gentleman—most urgent," the man apologized. Instantly the boy was on the alert.

"Who is it?" Through his brain raced the several unpleasant episodes of the past two days and he wasn't taking any chances.

"I do not know. He begs to see you."

"All right, come along down."

The two went to the front of the house where the boy saw a man who seemed very much distraught. He was pacing the floor in quick nervous strides, and as he held his hat in his hand, with his other hand he kept brushing back his hair, and jerking his arms as if the passing moments were matters of life and death. When Jim and the servant entered, the chap spun around on his heel.

"Pardon, pardon, senor—I am as one mad. You are not a father, you cannot know. I beg of you to help me—Please come—" The sentences were chopped off incoherently.

"Tell me who you are," Jim interrupted sharply.

"Gonzalas, that is my name. Pedro Gonzalas. I have been in America where you do things well, and are humane—"

"Suppose you sit down and tell me what you want," Jim invited. The servant drew up chairs, and the man sat on the edge of one, but he jumped up again immediately.

"I cannot sit quietly when my child is at death's door, senor. I beg of you to help me—"

"You'll have to tell me what you want."

"Yes, yes, your pardon. My child, we live in the mountains below the pass, and my child is dying. The doctor say something in the tube will save his life—I have the tube—but the hours are passing and I cannot drive home quickly enough. In the town they say you are an American, a clever man, and you have a plane. Please, I beg of you delay not. I will pay you well—"

"You mean that you want me to take the stuff to where your baby is?" Jim asked, any suspicion of the man completely dispelled by his very evident anxiety.

"Of a certainty," Gonzalas told him. "Please, my wife—it is our first born—he had the soft eyes like a fawn, and his life it is ebbing away from us—so helpless we are to save him."

"My brother has the plane and I don't expect him home for a couple of hours at least," Jim explained.

"Oh, my God!" The man flopped into the chair, buried his head on his arm and cried bitterly. "My little son," he moaned.

"But there are other planes in Cuzco," Jim reminded him. "You could telephone from here and I am sure that some one will take it for you."

"Three I have tried," the man sighed hopelessly. He gave the names of men who owned machines. "One, she has broken her wing, two she is far to the north, three leave one hour ago for Panama. Nothing I can do. Oh, my God, my little son!" Then, suddenly Jim remembered the De Castro's plane. He was positive they would have no objection to his taking it to save the child's life.

"How far is it?" he asked.

"One hundred and fifty miles. Senor, you have a good heart. You do not help because you cannot." He started to leave and his feet dragged as if they were weighted with lead.

"Just a minute. The folks here have a machine. I'll use that," he promised quickly. "Wait for me!" He raced up stairs, put his books and instruments out of harm's way, slipped into his aviation suit, and then hurried back to the distracted father who was fervently counting his beads as he murmured prayers of thankfulness. At the reappearance of the Flying Buddy, who looked like a young Viking, the man leaped to his feet, caught the lad's hand and embarrassed him indescribably by kissing it fervently.

"If Senor de Castro returns before I do, please explain where I have gone, and why," Austin said hastily to the manservant, who seemed glad that a way had been found to help the stranger.

"Si, senor," he agreed.

"Come along," Jim urged and the two made their way to the hangar where Pedro Gonzalas was settled in the seat beside the pilot. "You have your stuff all right?"

"Mother of God be praised, it is safe."

"Good." Jim made a hasty inspection of the plane, hopped into his own seat, and gave her the gun and they rolled out. She required considerably more space than the "Lark" before her wheels left the ground, but at last she lifted gracefully and began to climb bravely into the air. They went up in a wide curve which brought them three thousand feet above the De Castro homestead, the machine's nose screwing forward on an air-line for the well-known pass. Swiftly they thundered along, and then suddenly the man beside the boy wrote something on a piece of paper and handed it over because he knew nothing of the speaking tube.

"Cyat Pass," Jim read and this surprised him.

When Gonzalas had said that he lived 'below the pass' the boy had concluded that he meant the well-known one through the Andes. He glanced suspiciously at his companion, then he reasoned that the man's home was at Cyat Pass, or below it; the fact that he had failed to give the name was not surprising. The mountains were full of narrow highways going through one spur or range to another and to each locality they were of equal importance. But one thing did bother him. If there was any sort of treachery afoot the De Castros and Bob would start a search for him in the wrong place. He took the tube and motioned to his companion how to use it.

"Where is it?" he asked.

Gonzalas made a rough sketch on the back of an envelope, and after a few more questions, Austin understood. As they flew he recalculated his course, and although he had not revealed the correct destination at once, Jim was convinced that there was nothing criminal about the chap at his side. Gonzalas glanced at him with anxiety which was genuine but as they rushed forward he became more and more composed. Several times his eyes wandered over the globe rolling beneath them and as he seemed to recognize familiar landmarks he was apparently relieved. The first hour slipped by and during the second they were flying over a part of the country dotted with fertile plains and great plantations. Then they turned sharply and soared with a roar that the echoes took up as they rushed along near the ceiling while mountain ranges tipped out of their vision, very much as telephone poles do when watched from a rushing train, but not quite so fast. The second hour had gone by when Gonzalas, his eyes alert, pointed to series of foot hills.

"There are buildings on that plateau under the ledge," he announced.

"That where you want to come down?"

"Si, senor."

"That will be easy." Austin could see the rugged cliff and realized that getting through it from the ground would be a hazardous business. He surveyed the plateau, which had a few rough buildings such as formed hundreds of plantation or ranch homes, and a good road wound toward it from the back.

"It is four times so far by road," Gonzalas explained.

"Expect it is," agreed Jim. He selected a section which would afford the plane abundant room for the landing and then he noticed two men standing as if watching for the flyers. The motor was shut off and the machine began to alight.

"That is the doctor," Gonzalas told him. "My place is further in." This was another surprising bit of news and Jim scowled. The machine made a perfect landing, and the two men, both with bags, hurried to meet them. For a minute there was a swift exchange of conversation in Spanish and then Gonzalas turned to the boy. "The doctor must come to administer, and his helper. If you cannot carry so many, I shall get out, for they are to me important."

"Tell them to hop into the back," Jim directed.

"If you require gas there is some here," Gonzalas suggested.

"It will not be a bad idea to have it," the boy answered, so the extra supply was put in quickly.

Austin sized up the two passengers. One of them was short and slender, as if just past young manhood, but the other was mature. The medical man did not look like anyone else of the profession that Jim had ever seen, but there was nothing especially disturbing about any of them. They climbed into the back cock-pit, and were finally settled safely, then the plane rolled again, finally lifted the additional weight, and roared into the sky.

"I will direct you," Gonzalas explained.

"All right," agreed Jim. Although he was not afraid, he had a suspicion that all was not exactly as it should be and he determined to be on constant guard. He moved the mirror so that the occupants of the rear seat could be observed with little difficulty, and out of the corner of his eye he kept watch on Gonzalas. He had made up his mind that none of the passengers were air-men so at least he had that advantage over them if they made a false move. Half an hour passed, then the man beside him pointed ahead in a wide ravine.

"Beyond there."

Jim nodded and a few minutes later they were following the course of a river toward its source until they came to an abruptly rugged section. Here Gonzalas made careful observations, and after several minutes, pointed to the rim of the range, and motioned with his hands for Jim to follow that, which the boy did. At last they were nearing a small lake, the water of which appeared from that height to be very low, and on one side was a wide white beach. Austin wondered if the man's home was on the edge of the lake, but they flew across, then Gonzalas pointed out a narrow stream which almost looped in its winding twists as it made its way through the forest.

"Are we almost there?" Jim asked casually. "Don't want to come down here after it gets dark.

"Can you land there?"

Gonzalas pointed to a level spot that was quite low and dotted with vegetation, but the boy could see no sign of a habitation of any kind. However, it wasn't impossible for a home to be so situated that he had not picked it out, or it might be located further on where landing sites were less safe. He shut off the motor and they glided down on a long incline until finally they were standing still and as the boy glanced around he saw that they were in a sort of wide deep basin. His companion scrambled out quickly, and the two in the back seemed to be following his example, but there certainly wasn't a house in sight, nor any sign of one.

"We owe to you much, senor." It was the smaller of the two who had been in the rear, and Jim noticed that the chap's face was greatly troubled. "Please, permit me to speak with you and explain."

"Glad to have been able to get you here," Jim said heartily, and the fellow's eyes met his, then dropped.

"We—we have—what you call—played a trick on you, senor, but please I beg of you, listen and let me explain," he urged. Jim noticed that the other two had hurried away and the boy scowled.

"Well, why did you—"

"Please, patience. No harm, senor, shall come to you, only good, if you will listen."

"I'm all ears," Austin answered. The whole performance was mighty queer, but it certainly didn't look as if they had any evil intent.

"Gonzalas, he is my husband, and we have a little boy—one for whom we have great plans that his future may be big—not full of hardship." Jim stared, then chuckled inwardly because, of course, the smaller man was a woman. Being a Texan and a gentleman he hastily scrambled to his feet, and would have sprung to the ground, but he had another idea.

"Won't you sit here?" He pointed to the cock-pit, and she accepted.

"You are an honest boy, I know, and I shall tell you quickly, then you can decide what you will do," she smiled as he settled into his own place. "Weeks ago, my husband was lost in the forests, many days he wandered, sustaining himself on the roots and berries, which are many, and breaking his way until he could reach a settlement."

"Yes, I see." Jim was interested.

"In his school he studies the precious minerals, and he came to a place which attracted him very much. Senor, he found platinum; it is very valuable. He carefully marked the spot, stayed some time, and at last started again to find us. With him he brought a quantity of the platinum. He told no one his secret, but he took much which he sold in the north above Panama for a good price. He is returning—with me and his brother—and at Cuzo we learn rumors, doubted, but whispered from mouth to mouth, that platinum is found. This alarms us greatly, and we confer together. Many treacherous men would cut our throats, even kill our baby, to know of this spot my husband found, so we make a plan—you are an upright American boy, but to you we had to tell something false. May the Mother of God forgive us our sin—"

"You needn't feel badly about it," Jim hastily assured her.

"Thank you, senor. We have prepared a paper—what we find we will give to you an accounting and one-fourth of the mineral itself or we will pay you its value when it is sold," she said earnestly. As she talked she produced a number of folded papers which she opened and Jim saw an agreement which looked as if it were a perfectly legal instrument and at the end the three Gonzalas had put their signatures.

"You need not have done that," the boy said hastily.

"We wish you to be fully repaid," she smiled. "Put it in your pocket, and we will go."

"I ought to beat it back into the air," Jim hesitated.

"Before leaving you can see and tell my husband—shake with him the hand that you forgive the—false thing he tell to you," she pleaded so earnestly that it made Jim laugh to himself.

"All right," he agreed. They certainly were a queer bunch, not at all like many of the strangers he had encountered since his arrival in South America, but it was a mighty big relief to be assured that they were peaceful citizens; not out to kill him or anyone else. He hopped out of the plane, assisted Mrs. Gonzalas to alight, and she started toward a great boulder which they skirted.

"On this side is a small stream, which we follow; my husband told me the way many times," she explained with a smile.

The route was pretty rough, so Austin took her arm and helped her over the worst places, but she was so happy at their successful arrival that she hardly noticed the unevenness beneath her feet. In sections the brush was high and thick but the brothers had just broken through, leaving the way unmistakable, so the two proceeded until they reached a point where the river branched. Mrs. Gonzalas took the right turn and after ten minutes more travel, they came to a second fork, but water ran in only one of the beds. The woman plunged along the dry bed, scrambling so swiftly over the stones that Jim was sure she would stumble, but she was sure-footed. Presently they heard the voices of the men.

"Hello," Jim called.

"Helloo," Gonzalas responded quickly. He came toward them, followed by his brother, and Austin held out his hand.

"Glad I was able to help you," the Flying Buddy assured them.

"We pray for pardon for the sin," the brother put in quickly.

"And for your guardian angel ever to watch over you, for you were most generous," Gonzalas declared warmly.

"And the platinum, Pedro mio, it is here, si?" Mrs. Gonzalas was skipping about like a happy youngster and the two men exchanged anxious glances. "Show it to me," she urged.

"Patience, beloved one," Gonzalas urged.

"We seem not to find what we seek," his brother helped him.

"Not find it, mio? It is the river—the Platinum River we called it, with the forks, the dry bed—"

"Yes, everything—" Her husband shrugged his shoulders, then smiled cheerfully. "We are in the right place. We will search more careful. It could not—puff—be blown away."

V

PLATINUM RIVER

"Mio—Pedro— you would jest with me," Mrs. Gonzalas tried to laugh at the joke but it was a feeble attempt and she gave a little disappointed sob. "But this is the place. So many times you have told me, the river, small with three branches, one dry, and on that one you found the flakes— much— you brought much home; through the forests and over the mountains you carried it to us."

"Yes," the brother said dully, for Pedro looked at them all as if he had suddenly lost his reason or was a man asleep.

"I say, you probably got the wrong place, just a little off the course," Jim suggested. "Mind telling me how you marked it or remember where you found the stuff!"

"Si, senor. I am lost, wander in a circle, then I sleep and when I wake it is early morning. I wait for the sun—he is never wrong, then I start, resolved that due east I will go until I reach a stream. On a stream is always homes, settlements, maybe only trappers, but some one who will tell me how to go," he explained and he seemed glad to go into the details.

"Sure, I understand," Jim nodded.

"This stream I reach—nearer its source, and I follow with it to the fork. My mind is easy, I rest again and set some snares. For my dinner I get a rabbit and some fish with my hands. It is still day and I follow the water to the dry fork—and that I follow a mile and I find the platinum—quantities of it in the sharp sand."

"There is no sand here," Austin reminded him.

"None, but it is the dry fork—the only one," Pedro insisted.

"Maybe it isn't," Jim argued. "Why not have another look?"

"This is the only dry fork," Pedro answered.

"Did you tell anyone who might have come and got away with it?" Jim knew nothing about how platinum was found.

"That is impossible. I left great quantities, although I washed all I could carry in a bag I wove of the grass. This is a rocky place."

"That's right, but perhaps you passed it—"

"Impossible," the brother put in.

"Well, then it must be further along. You probably were so excited that you didn't notice how far you came. Didn't you leave a mark on the rocks or something?" Austin was mighty sorry for the little band and he couldn't make out how the place could be lost. The only thing he could think of was that Pedro had made a mistake in his reckoning, and being an air-man he knew any number of aviators did the same sort of thing and got miles out of their courses.

"I paced it," Pedro told him.

"You sure that you didn't tell anyone? Mrs. Gonzalas said that while you were in town—I mean Cuzco—that you heard rumors of platinum discoveries. She said that was why you told the fib so I'd bring you."

"That is true. At the fiesta many were drinking and two men talked of platinum over a table. Them I heard, and later I saw others whisper together, then hurry away—one left his wine."

"Great Scott, but there is no sign of anyone coming here."

"No one has been here. There is not a track but our own," said Pedro.

Well, now, come to think of it, while I was at the fiesta I heard a couple of men talking. One said that he had found platinum, but he didn't say where it was. He looked like a tough customer. Said that he had been in an airplane smash-up, the pilot was killed and this fellow wandered around for days before he dragged himself to a trapper's cabin. The hunter helped him get home, I mean to Cuzco, and he was put into a hospital. I don't know how long he was there, but he was positive he found platinum. Said that during the war he'd gone with a secret commission into Russia to get some so he knew it well. He was telling it to a fellow he was having lunch with. Did you see any airplane flying over while you were here, or see a smash-up?"

"No. Had I seen a plane I should have remembered for I should have concealed myself."

"Who was the man—do you know where he went?" Mrs. Gonzalas asked.

"As it happens, he was killed. I don't know the particulars, but I just told you about it because it proves that there must be a place where the mineral is and you have miscalculated. If you'd like me to, I'll go up in the air and look down through the glasses. I can soon spot the right dry fork for you and it will save no end of time," Jim suggested, and at that sensible idea they all brightened.

"It must be somewhere near, and perhaps—this is later in the season and more forks may have dried. It is many weeks since you were here," the brother suggested cheerfully.

"You are indeed a generous boy," Mrs. Gonzalas smiled. "Quickly you will find—" She stopped abruptly, for in the heavens somewhere near was a plane and it was flying low. Intuitively they all looked up and a moment later saw the machine like a great dragon-fly against the evening sky.

"Maybe I better wait until that lad gets out of the neighborhood," Jim suggested, for it suddenly occurred to him that it might be other men in search for the precious mineral.

"Let us conceal ourselves in the brush," Pedro whispered. "It will be better—safer." He helped his brother get Mrs. Gonzalas across the dry bed and up toward the rocks where a great patch of thick undergrowth would protect her from sight.

"Have you got any weapons—guns or anything?" Jim asked.

"This." Pedro produced a small but efficient automatic. "My brother, Arto—he has one larger, and a knife."

"Take this." Mrs. Gonzalas slipped a small gun and cartridges into Jim's hand and she seemed relieved to be rid of them. The lad judged by the look of astonishment on her husband's face that he did not know that she had them in her possession.

As they scrambled up the rock any noise

they made was deadened by the roar of the motor of the plane circling over their heads and Jim realized the Gonzalas probably anticipated some difficulty in maintaining their rights to the platinum they had found. He had read enough accounts of valuable discoveries in various parts of the world, and desperate struggles against unscrupulous men grimly determined to have at least a share in the wealth, regardless of whether their claim was justified, to appreciate the great importance of starting their enterprise well armed against attack. Being a Texas lad, Austin was familiar with fire-arms of various types, so a glance at the one the woman had given him, assured him that he understood its perfect mechanism. About half way up the ledge they reached an irregular section where a number of great stones looked as if they had been swept from the rim above and caught where they fell. All about them grew tough underbrush, some of it out of the crevices themselves, and this offered an excellent vantage point. No one could see them from the sky, get to them from behind, nor attack them from below without great difficulty.

"In here," Pedro urged his wife. He saw a triangular opening large enough for the woman to crawl in and be well protected.

"You will care take, mio," she said softly.

"Yes."

The brothers crawled to a second boulder close by but Jim climbed a bit higher and dropped down between two rocks which formed a barricade about him, yet gave him an excellent view of the dry bed and the vicinity. Although he had said nothing about it, he was mighty anxious about the De Castro's plane and was glad that it was parked some distance away, but he was fully aware that the pilot might very easily note its presence. By that time the airman had evidently selected a landing site, for the motor was shut off and the machine was gliding swiftly to earth. As it dropped, Jim scowled anxiously and thought soberly of the dangerous situation in which he and the Gonzalas were placed. The plane was none other than one of those used by members of the gang who had taken the Flying Buddies and the De Castros to Amy-Ran and endeavored to force from the boys some information regarding the activities of Don Haurea and his colleagues.

"If it's anyone from that gang, and the chances are that it is, I'm in for a hot time. They are sure to start a hunt for whoever came in the plane," the lad told himself soberly.

Carefully he watched the machine come down and he gasped with astonishment at the spot chosen. It was not far from where the Gonzalas had expected to find the platinum, and it was so wooded that the boy wondered how the pilot expected to pull out of it when they were ready to take the air again. When the machine stopped, three men hopped out, took a swift survey of their surroundings, then one of them started briskly toward the place where Pedro had stood a few minutes before trying to understand why he did not find the precious mineral he had left in the locality weeks before. It was apparent that the three men did not suspect they were not alone in that basin of the Andes mountains, for they rushed forward without caution, and this fact made Jim breath easier. He began to wonder why they had come and watched them narrowly, every faculty alert and tense. If anything happened to him, the Gonzalas would be in a mighty bad predicament. The men could make their way out to civilization but it would be a hazardous undertaking for the woman who appeared small and defenceless against such ruthless odds. This realization made the boy doubly careful not to disturb even a small stone that could attract the attention of the three below, who were now standing in the middle of the dry fork. The one man seemed to be surveying the locality with something of the same astonishment that Pedro Gonzalas had evidenced.

"Say, I knew this was a darn fool errand," snapped the smaller of the three, who, by his clothes, was apparently the pilot.

"It is not so," shouted the second man, whose clothes made him appear to be some sort of woodsman or hunter. "If you have come right, it is here."

"Well, I did come right," and then Jim had to brace himself, for there was young Arthur Gordon, whose ranch at the edge of Cap Rock in Texas was now deserted by the young outlaw who had managed to make endless trouble for Don Haurea and the Flying Buddies.

"There is no platinum here and there never was any," the third man announced positively, and then Jim had another shock, for this man was one of the chaps who had brought, or tried to bring, disaster to the power plant. His name was Alonzo and his brother had been killed along with a mysterious stranger only a week before. Their activities had branded them as criminals and the Peruvian government was anxious to get hold of him dead or alive.

"You could not have come right. I tell

you I copied the map from his wallet, exactly," the hunter insisted. Instantly it flashed into Jim's mind that this must be the trapper who had helped Ollie to civilization.

"Let me see it," growled Gordon. Alonzo took the folded paper from his pocket and the pair examined it carefully. "This is the place, all right. You've been made a goat. See? There's no platinum here."

"It is a trick," the trapper shrieked.

"You're a fool," Gordon bellowed and he doubled his fist threateningly.

"You would kill me and get the stuff yourself," the trapper accused as he backed away from them, but Alonzo, snarling furiously, leaped to catch him. With a move so swift that the boy hiding above could not follow it, the trapper threw a long glistening knife with such force and accuracy that it plunged into Alonzo's throat. He sank in a heap to the ground, gave a convulsive twist and lay still.

"You—" Gordon swore furiously, then suddenly he stopped. Instantly he seemed to forget the assault and his companion, and stood tense, his eyes turned toward the sky. In a moment the unmistakable hum of an airplane came to them. "My God—" He stepped quickly to the side of the dead man, gave him an indifferent kick with his foot, rolling the body over, pulled out the knife, which he threw to his companion, and deftly he went through the pockets for other weapons.

"You are going to kill me—"

"Shut up! Take this, we're going to have a heck of a fight on our hands and you'll need to use everything you can get to come out with a whole skin. See!" He tossed a revolver to the trapper, and cutting the cartridge belt from Alonzo's body, divided its contents, all the while looking about for some avenue of escape.

While Jim watched the movements of the two, his mind was busy trying to puzzle out the whole affair. It was apparent that Gordon had come expecting to find platinum. They had landed in almost exactly the same spot where Gonzalas was positive he had discovered it and the map, or whatever the trapper had copied from Ollie's wallet, must have given the same locality. Ollie had declared that he was sure of his find, and had made his identification with such care that Arthur had located the section from the plane. It was not possible, Jim reasoned, for both Pedro Gonzalas and Ollie to have made the same error in the calculations, yet there was no sign of anything of value in the vicinity. It was certainly puzzling, but the boy could not give the matter too much thought. With Gordon alone their position was dangerous enough, but with the coming of the second plane it looked as if other men had learned of the discovery and were bent upon getting possession of the land. Austin watched the two below, who were giving their undivided attention to the later arrivals, standing with weapons ready to repel attack and seemingly to have abandoned any idea of leaving the place without a fight.

"That bird's not coming down," Jim said softly to himself and drawing some of the foliage carefully above his head, he ventured stealthily to peep out.

The plane was executing a wide circle as low as the pilot dared in that rugged section, and the boy noticed that at least three men were staring over the sides of the cockpit. The machine dived swiftly toward the dried bed of the river-branch, leveled out precariously close, then with nose tilted, shot high and so close to the ledge that the boy could easily see the landing gear. He wondered why Gordon and the trapper did not run to shelter, or get away in their own machine, for it was obvious that they anticipated trouble. Perhaps he did not dare risk a smash-up if he attempted flight, for his machine was not in a position from which to make a hasty take-off; also, probably Arthur thought that concealment would serve him little, for his machine must have been spotted immediately by the men in the air. They were zooming swiftly and as steeply as they dared. For a moment Austin thought they were going to climb well out of the dangerous zone above the ledges and go away, but this idea was soon dismissed, for by the sound he could tell that the machine was circling again, and presently it came into view far below; diving as before, only this time, he saw one of the men high in his seat. Down it roared, the wheels barely escaping the topmost branches as it came like some bird of prey, the men straining forward with faces set and determined.

Something suddenly startled Gordon, for he jumped toward them as hard as he could go and in a ziz-zag course. He clutched the trapper as he passed, but the man stumbled, and almost at the same instant there was a flash of flame, followed by a vicious rat-a-tat-tat that sent a hail of shot in a wide swath. It cut the trapper down in a lifeless heap.

"A machine gun," Jim whispered. "Regular war stuff!" He was so fascinated that he could hardly take his eyes off the deadly instrument of destruction and it wasn't until bits of stone and rebounding bullets began to pepper the rocks where he and his friends were hiding that he backed further into the shelter of the boulders. He hoped fervently that the Gonzalas were well protected from the attack and he tried to calculate a way of helping his companions. He couldn't leave his own corner without risking being seen and that certainly would not help them.

From under his hiding place the boy listened intently and heard the plane going up again as if to repeat the maneuver, then suddenly it came back more quickly and its motor was shut off.

"They must be coming down," he told himself. Creeping close to the opening he made a place so that he could see what was taking place below and then he saw Arthur standing waving his white handkerchief. By that he knew that the young Texan was signaling his surrender. The machine descended quickly, presently landed, ran a few feet and stopped.

"What you doing here?" came a hoarse demand, as a man leaped from the cock-pit. He shoved his helmet back from his face and then Jim recognized the chap who had been with Ollie Boome at the fiesta, the man the police were so anxious to capture, and the same fellow who had circled above Amy-

Ran early that morning. It hardly seemed possible that so much could have happened in one day.

"I might ask you the same question," Gordon answered indifferently, "and I might add, what are you shooting the place up for?"

"You might, yes. Explanations are in order but they are coming from you. What are you butting into the chief's work for? This isn't the first time—"

"No? Well, the chief isn't taking me into his confidence these days so how the blazes could I know he was sending a bunch of you fellows here?" Arthur demanded hotly. He had taken a cigarette from his pocket and was lighting it coolly.

"Of course you didn't know—you or Alonzo—"

"Of course. You killed the two of them—the trapper and the big gun. That may require some explanation—"

"None of your funny business. What are you doing here? Why did you come?" the man snapped.

"Probably for the same reason you did, but I don't know how we all happened to land in this place," Gordon answered. "Alonzo came to me with the hunter and said they wanted me to fly them to a place where platinum had been found. The trapper had a map, it's here on the ground somewhere, but I don't know how you got wind of the same thing."

"It's none of your business. You'd better get into your machine and report to the chief. He's got a job for you—"

"You need not be so anxious to get rid of me—"

"Aw, come on, let's give him the works; he's always balling things up," one of the other men proposed.

"There's nothing here to ball up, old timer. We're a lot of goats, somebody's—"

"Goats, what do you mean?"

"There's no platinum here, that's what I mean. Have a look for yourself. There never was any here," Gordon told them. Instantly the men began to look about the section, and those who had flash-lights turned them on, for it was beginning to get dark.

"It's some of his funny business, I'll bet. He's just making fools out of us again, or trying to, but he doesn't play that game twice with me—not me." One of the men stepped quickly to Gordon's side and swung his fist, but the Texan's foot shot out and the fellow went sprawling.

VI

CAPTURE

"Any of you other men want what's coming to you?" Gordon snarled as he stood over his victim, a black automatic in each hand. The men who were advancing menacingly on him stopped in their tracks and swore furiously.

"Keep your shirts on, all of you," the leader snapped. "You fellows want to remember that I am running this picnic and you are here to obey orders. Gordon, put up those irons or I'll rake you with the machine gun." As he spoke the one man who had remained in the plane rose in the cock-pit and swung the shiny nose of the weapon on the group.

"He's such a liar," one growled.

"I've told you the truth," Gordon answered and his face was dark, but he slipped the guns in his pockets.

"You can hardly blame the boys for doubting your word."

"I do blame them, Cardow; I've told you the truth."

"You said that you came here with Alonzo and that trapper. Who else came with you?" Cardow demanded.

"No one, I tell you. The only reason they brought me was because I could fly the plane," Arthur declared hotly.

"Who owns the other plane?" Cardow asked.

"What other plane?"

"Aw, Cardow, listen, this guy is always in the works—he butts in— and he's always the one that gets away and some other guys hold the bag," one of the men argued.

"Yeh. We come up here and find him, the two guys with him dead as a canned cod, and he says the platinum ain't here. What the blazes did he do with it?"

"That bozo wasn't talking through his hat when he told you he found it," the men put in persistently.

"You shot the trapper—"

"But not Alonzo," came the sharp interruption.

"No, but he started to fight with the trapper and the fellow knifed him. You can see by the wound if you've got sense enough to tell a gun hole from a blade," Gordon shot back; then he turned to Cardow. "I don't know what you mean by another plane—"

"Well, there's one sitting pretty not a mile

from here—crate flying," the man roared at him.

"Another plane—well, if there is, this is the first I've heard about it," Gordon declared emphatically.

"Didn't you see it while you were flying?"

"Don't be a fool! Do you suppose if I had I should not have found out about it? I didn't see it and I didn't see anyone belonging to it."

"Maybe it's one of those police guys that's been broadcastin' your pitcher so handsome, Cardow," a man suggested with a grin.

"If it is, Jo, you're as good as in a Peruvian prison for being found with me," Cardow reminded him coldly, and the grin disappeared.

"G'wan, if it was a police guy he'd a been here long ago to know 'bout the fire-works."

"Sure, Brick's right," Jo responded with relief.

All of this Austin heard from his hiding place high above them while his brain was making a furious effort to plan a means of escape for himself and his friends. If he could get them, under cover of the growing darkness, to the machine, they would have a fighting chance of getting into the air before the bandits could start their own planes and give chase. Cautiously he leaned further forward, and then he heard one of the men again arguing against Gordon.

"Listen, Cardow, Gordon here is at the Amy-Ran works. We had those prutty-jays of the Don's tied handsome, me en Carp here a watchin' 'em fer Gordon, en he shows up late like a dibbytant stidda bein' on time—"

"Yeh," Carp interrupted, "he's holdin' up the works, and when—"

"You can leave out names, Carp," Cardow snapped.

"Sure, yeh. Well, when the partner comes along he give Gordon here the devil and we didn't git nothin' outta the hull night's work—"

"Do you think I set that mountain spouting?" Gordon roared at him.

"No, but I think you ain't none too unfriendly with that other gang, see, fer if youda been on time we'd a got something done before it began to shoot its head off," Jo snarled.

"Well," volunteered Carp, "I'm tellin' you it didn't shoot its head off, er nothin' of the kind. Ain't that so, Cardow?"

"Yes it is, but there is going to be some real fireworks there to-night, and we're going to be there—"

"What do you mean it didn't shoot off—the

volcano, I mean?" Gordon demanded. "I was there—saw it hit the sky—"

"It was a trick of some kind. I flew over the place this morning and there's no sign of a volcano, or any sort of eruption. I examined the place with glasses and I know what I'm talking about. But, there's one thing about it and as you are coming back with me you may as well know—and no funny business—that Amy-Ran cliff, or whatever it is called, *is* the place where the treasure is hidden. If it hadn't been there, they would not have made such an attempt to be rid of all of you. It is clear enough that the people were ready for a search of the locality and used that means of driving them off. I've got men today well under cover, laying a whole string of dynamite that will open it up wide and we're going to be on hand when the spark goes off. Understand?"

"No, I don't," Gordon answered in a puzzled tone.

"I admit that volcano was a good trick; but it was good for us, too. Now, we'll get out of here—"

"But how about the platinum?" Jo put in quickly. "I think this guy knows where it is."

"Well, he doesn't. There's been some fluke about that map. I know the fellow

Boome found the stuff, all right, so we'll get men here in the daytime and find the right location," Cardow told him.

"Suits me. Say, can we eat?"

"Yes, there's time, and there are a couple of other things we have to do before we start. If you make a fire, be careful that it's hidden from the sky—"

"Sure."

"Senor Jim—" Pedro Gonzalas' coming had been accomplished so quietly that Austin almost jumped out of his skin at the soft call.

"Here." In a moment Pedro crawled close, wriggling like a snake around the rocks, which were now covered with deep shadows.

"Come," he urged, so Austin prepared to follow. It seemed to the boy that they went by inches, but presently they had wormed their way back along the ledge, and there he found Arto and Mrs. Gonzalas. He wondered a moment how they had succeeded in getting there, but there was no time to ask questions.

"Step with care," Arto whispered, and the four started as quickly as possible into a narrow route that zig-zagged behind some of the tallest stones, and presently they reached a thick wood, which they entered. The trees grew tall and close together, but there was little underbrush so they made excellent progress, and finally when they paused for breath, they were some distance from the basin and its murderous occupants.

"Have you a pocket compass?" Pedro asked.

"Sure," Jim replied quickly, for he always carried a small one that he used when he wasn't flying. "Want me to set a course to the plane from here?"

"If you can. You will have to keep out of sight of the riverbed, but it curves just above where we were hiding, like a horseshoe, so we do not need to cross. When I camped here, I investigated that much because I knew it was well to familiarize myself with the locality," Gonzalas explained.

"Good you did. Gosh, we were in a tight hole a while ago, but we're not out of it yet," he said softly, and by the aid of a match he studied the tiny instrument which would help them take a direct course. Recalling the place where they had landed, he soon calculated which way they should go.

"Come along," he smiled.

"I think we can safely use a little light," Arto suggested. He produced a small pocket flash, and the four started.

There was so much that Jim had overheard from the platinum hunters that his brain was in something of a turmoil, and he had two reasons for being anxious to get away as quickly as possible. Besides getting the Gonzalas to safety, he wanted to get a warning to Ynilea of the threatened attack, in case Cardow's operations had by any chance escaped the attention of the Laboratory men. However, his immediate job was to lead his friends to the plane and get them away safely, if that was possible. Once in the air, they could shoot through the sky and get out of range of the machine gun, if Cardow gave chase.

Jim reasoned that the gang leader, or lieutenant, probably did not know either of the Flying Buddies, and the fact that he had not been seen near the supposed platinum deposit might make him unsuspicious, but the boy fully expected that when the plane took the air, at least the one with the machine gun would come up to investigate and make sure who was in it. The possibility of his not being recognized was mighty slim, but he hoped to get away too quickly for them to overtake him, in case Gordon should catch a glimpse of him. The boy dismissed the thought, for he knew perfectly well that his Texas neighbor would prove a nasty customer. As they proceeded, he mentally calculated the course he would take when they got into the air, if they did. He could start directly away from the gang plane or planes and that would give him a bit of advantage, but he wished with all his heart that it was the "Lark," instead of De Castro's plane he had with him.

"I smell cooking—bacon frying," Mrs. Gonzalas sniffed the air and in a moment Jim too got a whiff of the appetizing fragrance, for the wind brought it directly to them.

"That's a sign they are busy," he said softly.

"You must be hungry. I have something in my pocket." She produced a generous square of chocolate and a sandwich rolled in oiled paper.

"That looks great, but you had better eat it," he urged her.

"We did eat some in the cave," she smiled.

"Sure?" he demanded.

"Sure—we each save something for you—and forget to give it," Pedro told him contritely. "We are—the un-rich sports."

"You're all right," Jim grinned and accepted the offering, which he ate as they hurried along. Although they felt somewhat confident that the men in the basin were occupied for the moment, they took no chances, and at last, after a wide detour, they saw the great stone a short distance away from them.

"You, my wife get to the machine. Arto and I will go around and look for enemies, please."

"Good stunt," Jim whispered.

"For danger, we will whistle softly. My wife knows the call." Pedro put his hand on Jim's arm. "To you we owe much, today, senor. Could you get my wife away—go—do not wait for us," he pleaded.

"I'll do my best to get you all away—"

"But if you cannot—do not wait. We have a little boy—he should not lose his mother, please."

"All right," Jim gulped hastily. In a moment the brothers had disappeared in the shadows, and Austin, gun in one hand, Mrs. Gonzalas' wrist grasped firmly in the other, proceeded as cautiously as a pair of panthers. Step by step they went, slowly drawing nearer to the machine and no warning whistle reached their ears. They had nearly reached it when Jim paused to listen. He thought he heard a twig break, but only the sighing of the wind broke the silence of the night. Glancing over his shoulder he watched, but nothing stirred, then they took another step.

"Mother of God watch over us," the woman prayed, scarcely above her breath and the words gave Jim a new sense of confidence.

"When we get to the fuselage I'll boost you on. Be as quiet as you can, and drop into the cock-pit without raising up if you possibly can," he whispered, for all of a sudden Jim had a life-sized hunch that Cardow would have someone watching the plane.

"God guard you," the woman answered. Like a pair of shadows they advanced and reached the end of the wing; step by step they took, only a few inches at a time, until they were beside the body of the plane. Jim stooped and cupped his hand and Mrs. Gonzalas put her foot into it. Carefully he raised her as she braced, then she gave a spring and drew herself upward. Again Jim paused and listened, with gun in hand, then he leaped up beside the woman, who was sliding into the forward cock-pit. In a moment he ducked low and switched on the smallest dial light, which was just sufficient to read the control board.

"Keep down," he told her quietly, but his heart was beating like a trip hammer. He made his calculations swiftly, listening the while for the approach of the brothers, or the warning whistle of danger. He was mighty thankful that the climate was mild and that the engine would not require a lot of warming up. He set everything possible while he waited, then he heard swift steps and glancing to the right, he saw Arto running. A second later the man sprang on the front of the machine, and at the same time, there came the warning whistle.

Mechanically Jim gave her the gun and flashed on the lights, which revealed Pedro, a bit to the left, racing toward them. Then out of the darkness into the light leaped the ugly forms of Joe and Carp who were close on their victim. The plane moved forward.

"My husband, they will kill him," the woman shrieked, but her brother-in-law had thrown himself flat across the plane, his arms outstretched as they rolled forward.

A series of shots spat from the guns of Carp and Joe, but Pedro leaped, the plane lunged sidewise, and just before she lifted from the ground, Arto caught his brother's hands and held them tight. Then, to Jim's horror, Mrs. Gonzalas was over the rim of the cock-pit, her body thrown against Arto's to help him hold his precious burden. Up the plane climbed, and as she soared, Austin got a rope from the equipment box and looped the end. One hand on the stick, the young Texan shot the lasso forward and low, then with a deft twist he brought it up, pulled it tight, and taking an instant to glance over the side, he sighed with relief when he found that it was really around Pedro's waist. Jim tied the other end to one of the braces, then gave his undivided attention to flying, for the acrobatic stunts and the uneven distribution of the weight were making the machine climb crazily. In a few minutes he had her well under control, and a bit later, Mrs. Gonzalas, her face pale with fright, slid back to her seat. Presently Arto too climbed over the cock-pit, his lips set, and behind the pilot, he assisted his brother to safety. In a little while the pair of them were in the rear cock-pit, and all was well, for the enemy was far behind.

When they had started, Jim had intended to turn away from the direction of the basin, but he had not been able to accomplish this at once, so he was beyond the ledge where the gang had hidden before he could set her course, so now he shot straight ahead. Occasionally he glanced back for a sight of the machine which would surely take after them, and once, for an instant, he shut off the motor. They were in the air all right, so the boy climbed high and quickly, his lights doused; then he did a wide circle back hoping to get on the tails of his pursuers. As he spiraled he drove through a thick cloud bank which spread its shelter about them, but the air got biting cold, and the boy was afraid the woman beside him would suffer. She wore a man's suit and a coat, but he wasn't sure how warm she was.

"Keep low," he urged her, so she slid forward in the seat. Then he remembered that the De Castros always carried extra coats under the pilot's seat, so he fished them out, and proceeded to wrap her up warmly, just as he and Bob wrapped Mrs. Austin when she joined them in an air joy-ride.

"That is good," she smiled, and presently her lips looked less blue and he knew that she was more comfortable. He tipped the plane's nose again and shot up, then he leveled off, set his course, and calculating that the machines that were chasing him would be lower and ahead of him, he strained to see through the darkness. It wasn't a moonlit night, but there were stars that helped some as they soared close to the ceiling.

Half an hour passed, then Jim was beginning to feel confident that they had successfully eluded Cardow and his gang, but he did not turn on a light lest someone pick them up.

"Know anything about the towns around here?" he asked his companion.

"No," she answered. He had planned that he would come down in one of the small settlements and send messages to the De

Castros that he and the plane were quite safe, and he thought it would be better to get Mrs. Gonzalas to the ground as soon as possible. She certainly was a plucky little woman. They were a mighty decent family, Jim thought, and again he wished he was at the controls of the "Lark" whose speed was so much greater.

"Is your home in Cuzco?" he asked.

"Yes, not far outside. A small place," she told him.

"Reckon I'd better get you there," Jim remarked. "Ever fly before?"

"Never until today."

"Like it?"

"It is beautiful—so beautiful," she answered. "If the platinum had been there, a plane we should have had. Arto, in the war he fly, but he is injured. No more is he a good pilot, but he is mechanic for the transportation company, and sometimes he relief."

This surprised Jim, for he thought that neither of the brothers was an air man, and then he realized that the scheme to get him to carry them was more like something a flyer would concoct than a layman. He grinned to himself as he thought of the simplicity of the plan, and then he sobered. It had brought him into a dickens of a mess, to be sure, but he thought that he was mighty lucky it was the Gonzalas who had come after him. Any member of the gang might have sprung the same story and he would have been taken in just as quickly.

"Reckon I'm not such a Jumbo of intellect," he remarked to himself.

"Oh," the woman clutched his hand, "look!" At that moment the plane was bathed in a flood-light from another machine shooting directly above them. "God have mercy!"

VII

THROUGH SPACE

The sudden appearance of the plane flying directly over their heads with its flood light pouring on them made Jim's heart skip a beat. So much time had lapsed since the four had taken off, in spite of the activity of Joe and Carp, that the Flying Buddy had begun to feel confident that the danger of pursuit was passed, but now he knew that he had reckoned prematurely and his greatest anxiety was for the woman who was crouching in terror beside him. Mechanically he put out his hand to assure himself that her safety strap held her firmly and he knew that her parachute was properly adjusted. Without moving in his own seat he pressed the button that signaled for the attention of the two men in the rear cock-pit, and in a moment he heard Arto's voice in his ear.

"We are here," the man said tensely.

"Strapped tight?"

"Si, senor."

"Good. Chutes on?"

"Si." Jim was glad that this Gonzalas brother had been an airman, for of course he would see that he and his brother were not taking undue risk during the long flight through the night.

"Fine. Hang on!"

"The sister?"

"She is top hole," Jim assured him.

"Bravo! We are the fruit!"

"Berries," Jim had to chuckle.

"Si. Gooseberries maybe, but we are present. Can I assist?"

"Don't know. Keep your ear plastered to the tube and leave the connection on. Also, watch what I do and be prepared to follow if necessary," Jim answered briefly, then he smiled confidently at his companion and some of his spirit gave her renewed courage.

Up to that moment Cardow's plane had made no overt move but continued in the course and kept its light, which was surprisingly brilliant, on the machine below it. Jim wondered what they looked like from the ground and if anyone happening to observe them would think of danger. For a moment he did nothing but fly straight, then suddenly he tipped the plane's nose at a sharp angle and began to climb so swiftly that the menacing plane would be forced to slacken its speed or risk a collision, for Jim was shooting directly into its track. Up he zoomed and in a moment had shot beyond the rim of light, which apparently was not a revolving one and that fact was some comfort, but the boy had to blink quickly when he climbed through the intensified darkness.

Keeping his eyes on the plane still above him Jim realized that the pilot either was not calculating the point ahead where the two machines would come to grief, or else the man considered the Flying Buddy's maneuver a bluff and expected that the smaller plain would scoot out of the path of destruction at the last moment. By that time Austin could see the two men in the forward cockpit and suddenly he saw the man next the pilot rise as high in his seat as straps permitted and his mouth opened to its fullest capacity as if he were shrieking a warning. Not until then did the second machine tip its nose upward and veer slightly from its course so that Jim and his companions rushed like a rocket above them.

Glancing at the altimeter, Austin saw that he had climbed nearly two thousand feet and out of the corner of his eye he saw the gunner on the gang's plane swing his deadly weapon onto its standard and stand ready to send a round of bullets into them the instant they flew across his sight. There was no doubt of their evil intention and Jim's mind worked fast. Below them was the rugged rim of one of the ranges of the Andes mountains, and far ahead, the boy knew there were deep sandy plains. Any kind of landing where they were would mean a smash-up and his passengers, if they were not killed outright, would surely be badly injured, so he made up his mind that he would keep in the air as long as he could.

Austin wished heartily that some of them had weapons of longer range so they would have a chance in a gun fight, but only the luckiest sort of sharp shooting would avail them anything in their present predicament. If the light was not a revolving one the machine gun was, he knew, and for him to fly close enough to get in a shot that would cripple the pilot would mean that the woman crouched beside him, and probably all of them, would be raked with vicious bullets which would put an end to them speedily. Some queer streak in his brain made him think of Pedro's earnest plea to save his wife at least so their little son would not be motherless. Austin had lost his own mother when he was a boy and he remembered vividly the awful loneliness without her. To be sure, he had Dad, who was the best yet, and later Dad had married Bob's mother, who had almost succeeded in making her step-son forget that he wasn't her own "born-boy," but step-mothers as a general rule do not turn out so well, but yet, if Pedro were killed the little lad waiting in Cuzco would be mighty forlorn.

"We've got to get out of this," Jim said grimly to himself. He was still climbing and the second plane was following close on his trail, and its gunner had an eye cocked to his weapon. Banking sharply, Jim curved to the right, then executed a half loop which brought him up behind his enemy. Climbing a few rods he managed to get his plane's nose so dangerously close to the tail of the other, that its pilot tried to shake him by dropping a bit and making a curve, but the Flying Buddy was tensely alert and kept after the machine, realizing that for the moment he had the advantage. He did not forget to keep a watchful eye on the control board and dials so that he would not be led out of his course.

"Another plane is coming," Arto spoke in his ear.

"Which way?"

"Below and behind," Arto answered. "I just saw it, but it has no lights I can see."

"Thanks."

Certainly the situation was not improving.

Glancing ahead and above the boy saw some dark clouds forming, and when his eyes returned to the enemy plane, he realized that its pilot was looping down and intended to come back on his tail. The maneuver was a good one, as Jim knew, but in this case it would mean a few second's delay, so ignoring their pursurers, he put on every ounce of additional speed and raced for the protection of the thick mist. In a moment its moisture was on their faces, then Jim dived low, leveled off and shot forward. He was mighty thankful they had the extra tanks of gas Pedro had supplied and making a hasty calculation he figured they could keep in the air many hours. His watch told him that it was nearly half past ten and he recalled that Cardow had said he was going to be present at the dynamiting of Amy-Ran. Taking his bearings carefully, then estimating the distance to the ancient fortress, Austin knew that it would require forty minutes at least for the gang to reach their destination so they had little time to waste trying to bring him down. If he could possibly dodge them for fifteen minutes, they would probably give up the chase; that is, unless the second machine was detailed to keep after him.

Flying through the blanket, blind and unable to hear the enemy planes was nerve-racking, so Jim zoomed upward and when he had gained two thousand feet he put his machine into a glide and listened. For a moment he heard nothing, then he realized that probably the other pilots were doing the same thing, but he had the advantage of having shut off his motor last and he hoped they would be compelled to start their engines before he did and give him an idea of their locality. He reasoned that they were flying close together for they must have signaled to each other. According to the chart in front of him he was still over the rugged mountain section and his eyes rested anxiously on the altimeter. If it was faulty they were out of luck.

"Have we escaped from them?" Mrs. Gonzalas asked.

"I'm trying to find out. Do you hear them?" She listened earnestly endeavoring to help.

"A rushing noise, maybe like we make with our wires," she suggested.

"Which way do you get it?"

"As if it comes from lower." They sat quietly and then Jim to picked up the sound but he calculated that it was an echo from below and that might be started from their own plane. He maneuvered with the air currents, which were rushing and rolling the mist, and managed to sail forward, then he continued the glide. They had settled fifteen hundred feet, and there was still no sign of a break.

"If they come up—" Arto spoke softly through the mouthpiece and Jim pressed it closer to his ear, "could we use the guns?"

"You might get a chance. Are you a good shot?"

"Crack," Arto answered. "Pedro, too, he is—very better—good."

"All right, take a pop at them."

"Mrs. Gonzalas, is she in fear?"

"They want to know if you are afraid," Jim told her, so she raised her head a bit and spoke into the mouthpiece.

"I am not afraid for I pray the Mother of God for her protection. Mio! You and Arto are safe?"

They answered in Spanish, and she smiled with satisfaction, then the conversation was stopped abruptly by the sputter and roar of a motor which seemed close at the left and above them.

"Thanks, old timer," Jim grinned.

He opened his own motor and shot up, climbing steadily until he was four thousand feet higher, and there he came out above the clouds. Here he shut off the engine and gliding quietly, listening to the commotion made by the machines below. Before they slipped down to the cloud ceiling, Jim started the motor again and soared along in exactly the opposite direction from their course. In this way the Flying Buddy hoped to rid himself of Cardow and his gang. Just beneath them the clouds were rolling, some of them with light tips made silver by the moon which had come out like a beautiful glowing ball that dimmed the stars. Mrs. Gonzalas gazed about her with lips parted in awe and wonder, and she even ventured to peep over the side at the marvelous panorama. Occasionally they passed open places and could see the sleeping globe with here and there a few feeble lights about a building or on a road winding through the mountains. The scene was so vast and wonderful that is seemed more like an amazing dream than anything real.

"When we were flying this afternoon did your brother-in-law show you about the parachute?" Jim asked her.

"Si. Jump, fall a moment and pull the ring upper."

"That's right. Don't expect we are going to have to jump and if we do I'll keep with you, but it's just as well to be prepared."

"Those men go to the fastness rocks, they say," she responded.

"Yes, and we are sailing directly away from it, the opposite direction. Cardow can't chase us and get there on time," he explained assuringly.

"Maybe one plane will not give up," she suggested and Jim was mighty sorry that she had thought of that probability, but after all it was just as well that she realized they were not out of danger.

By that time they were miles out of their course and bringing the plane's nose about the Flying Buddy reset his route toward Cuzco. Studying the chart he saw that they would soon be traveling over valleys and that there were a few scattered settlements in the neighborhood. He had never happened to come down near any of those they would pass over, and he hesitated about making a landing lest the gang, which he knew was well organized, should have men posted on the watch for them to come out of the sky. He considered landing on one of the plantations, but he might pick the very one where gang-operators had a hang-out. After all, he decided, probably the best course was to keep flying, so he increased the speed and roared forward into another cloud bank. In its protection he listened a few minutes but not a sound came to him and with a sigh of relief he opened her up again. At least they had thrown off the other fellows for a while.

"Wonder what I'd do in their place," he asked himself, and then he did his reasoning along those lines. Assuming that the men were determined to capture him he was not long in reaching the conclusion that they would surely fly toward his destination as soon as they lost him in the clouds, and probably they would have men stationed on watch for him at scattered points; places where messages could be sent out. It was more than likely that the bigger of the two machines was equipped with radio and could be quickly informed of their whereabouts.

"Gosh, if this were only the 'Lark'," he sighed, but it wasn't and he felt as helpless in the machine as if he were in the midst of a squadron of planes. He thought about Bob and wondered idly how long he had remained at Amy-Ran and if the new radio had been installed. He knew a little about its capabilities and hoped that the night's adventure would not end so badly that he would never fly the loved machine again. Thinking about his Flying Buddy he suddenly straightened. When Bob reached home he would inquire for his side-kick the very first thing and when Jim didn't appear, the younger boy might go raring in search of him. There was some hope in the possibility, and then Jim recalled that the Pass he was supposed to go to with Gonzalas was nowhere near the one to which he really went. At that moment, Bob was probably flying hundreds of miles away.

"A plane comes from the right," Arto spoke into his ear. Jim looked quickly and a moment later picked out the machine rushing across a patch of light directly toward them. Mechanically he tipped up, zoomed without leaving his course, and then he saw a second machine tearing some distance from the first. They were both headed his way and as he climbed, the other pilots soared up swiftly and began to close in with an unmistakably vicious purpose. For a moment he thought of turning again, but changed his mind. He would make them turn instead, so he opened her up and rushed on, the wires whistling a shrill protest.

"If we come close, Pedro and I are ready with the guns," Arto said grimly, and Jim, with teeth set and body almost rigid, watched every move. Once he glanced back over his shoulder and just as he did his heart gave a leap, for a third plane was racing up from behind.

"Are they coming?"

"Three, all together," Jim told her and his lips were set.

"Why should they be so obsessed—so determined to kill us?"

"Reckon your husband was sort of foolish to ask me to fly him. There is a gang of chaps who have been raising heck with my father and me too. They probably know that I am flying his plane and have made up their minds to get me," he explained, then added, "I'm sorry you are in such a hole."

"We did not mean to place you in danger," she said anxiously. "It is not then just because of the platinum that they chase us?"

"Can't be, unless they think we found it." He moved the speaking tube to attend more strictly to business. There were no clouds to help them and Jim glanced at the chart. In a little while they would be above the plain out of the way of the rugged hills where coming down was so terribly dangerous. Keeping alert and watching tensely he held the stick, his left hand on the control board, and saw the two machines coming closer together with his own nose pointed directly between them. On and on they went, then he banked sharply and veered to the right so that he would pass on the outside of the pair, and with a quick twist, he zoomed higher and tore on, leveled off and raced forward. A minute later he had passed the first machine, and he glanced over his shoulder, but the third one was almost on his tail.

"Let him come up," Arto said in his ear, so the Flying Buddy decreased his speed somewhat, glancing back to see just how close the other fellow was coming.

"Crack! crack!" Two shots spat out from the rear cock-pit, and almost immediately two more. Again Jim glanced back and he saw that the nearest machine was still tearing almost upon him. Four more shots rang out from the guns of the Gonzalas', then the nearest plane wobbled as if the pilot had been hit.

"You have a gun," Mrs. Gonzalas shouted. "Give it to me, I can shoot it." He fished it out of his pocket and handed it over, looking first to be sure that it was ready for use.

They tore on and Jim saw the woman holding the weapon efficiently in her hand and was glad to see that she had been taught to handle it. On they went, and then, he saw a machine racing almost beside him. The guns cracked again but as far as the boy could see they did no real damage but it flashed through his mind that the pilots were not alarmed at the firing. They merely kept out of range.

"One is mounting his machine gun—on the right," Arto announced.

Jim glanced about and saw that this was so and he knew that in a moment they would be racked with a hail of lead. He tipped his nose down to a sharp angle, and dived steeply a thousand feet, leveled off and went on. It seemed to the boy as if he had been flying for an eternity and they would never get anywhere. They had nearly reached the plain and he took a survey about him. The plane with the machine gun was almost directly over him.

"Hang on," he yelled, then did a backward loop and as they came up he could see two of the machines rushing some distance ahead, but the third one was right beside him. Crack, went the Gonzalas' guns from the rear, and crack, crack, crack, came a fusillade from the pursuer, but it wasn't a machine gun. One shot splintered the rim of the forward cock-pit, and again Jim dived.

"Duck," he roared to his companion, fearing that she would be hit by a bullet. He couldn't expect to dodge forever, for one well directed shot would cripple the plane he was flying. The two planes were circling back, and Jim did another loop; coming up behind the three of them then he zoomed at top speed toward the ceiling, for each dive had made his position more dangerous. He could see the others start to follow but he went on at top speed, and soon he was well up in the heavens, where the pale stars seemed to blink in puzzled wonder at the desperate struggle going on under their noses.

The meter read twenty-thousand feet before the Flying Buddy brought the machine into a less steep angle, but he still climbed. Calculating hastily he found they were only slightly out of their course, then at thirty-thousand feet, he leveled off and rushed forward. Glancing back he was delighted to see that he had gained considerably on the other machines, but they showed no inclination to stop. The boy wondered if the firing would attract the attention of anyone below, but even if it did he could hardly expect help to reach him.

"They are gaining, two of them. The third seems not so swift," Arto informed him. Their own plane was going at top speed, and couldn't be forced any more swiftly.

VIII

THE AIR BATTLE

"Did you get any of them with your guns?" Jim asked.

"A splinter, perhaps," Arto answered.

The Flying Buddy made a swift survey of his surroundings, a glance at the dials in front of him and at the map. His brain was clear and worked with the precision and co-operation of the brave little machine he was driving through space. The whole affair seemed unreal, more like a horrible nightmare than an actuality, this endless flying to get away from men who were grimly determined to send him to destruction. He could see that the two swifter machines were gaining steadily, and had it not been for the woman beside him, Jim's anxiety would not have been so great, but somehow she must be saved. The only plan he could form was to keep in the air as long as he could. They were far from any sort of settlement which could give them shelter. From the ground the three men might fight it out with the enemy and have a slim chance, but with Gonzalas' wife to be considered, landing was out of the question. She might not be able to dig in quickly enough, so as long as the wings held up, they would fly, and of course, every second was bringing them a bit nearer to safety, but it was like crawling.

Crack, bang, a shot struck the fuselage at the right, and with a swift kick at the rudder, a bank with the wind which was rising, and a tilt of the nose, they began to climb again in short spirals which made them a poor target. Perhaps they might inveigle the gang to use up their ammunition, but that was hardly possible; they probably carried enough to bombard a town. The boy wondered if Cardow was with the gang or if he had gone on to the ancient fastness leaving his lieutenants to finish the Gonzalas. Jim had a hunch that young Gordon was in one of those planes and that was the reason the chase had not been abandoned. Up he climbed, then he noticed that the swifter machine was coming right along after him, the second followed, both driving in ascending circles not quite so tight as those Austin was making and he felt a bit as if he were in the middle of an old-fashioned bed-spring. They climbed faster and the third machine, which carried the machine-gun, was zooming like a shot.

"One is under us," Arto spoke in his ear.

"Thanks." With a quick flip Jim tipped his nose straight downward and with engine wide open he cut through the air like a rocket so furiously that the machines below him ducked to get out of his way. Neither of the pilots dared risk such a collision, and Austin was not sure that he would not pull out himself, but they scattered as he came, hell bent, and below them he leveled, shot back on his course, turned tail as it were, over the way he had come. It did not take the three long to get after him, then the boy began to climb, zooming so that the wires shrieked in the wind and wings groaned under the assault. He gained two thousand feet, then whirled so short that Mrs. Gonzalas was flung against him.

"All right," she smiled, but it was a mighty forced smile and the lad admired her pluck.

"If the little kid is like her he must be a rip-snorter," was his mental comment. He saw that his enemies were so close together when he made the maneuver they had to make a wide turn or collide with each other. That gave the Flying Buddy a few brief moments to gain distance and glancing over the side he saw that they were within a few miles of the plain which lay like a long ribbon of light sand beyond the edge of the foot hills. He put on a bit more speed and in a minute they were over the sandy stretch which would make a better landing place than the jagged mountains, unless he happened to come down on one of the vast stretches of cactus which dotted the desert. He knew that there were great beds of the low growing plant with small leaves but long, sharp thorns; also there were acres of giant plants as tall as trees with blades strong and sharp as sword points.

Soon the enemy ships were flying at him in a sort of military formation, and close together. They were probably signaling messages and a plan of attack for they must know that the Flying Buddy would slip through their fingers if he got away with many more tricks. On they came and they spread out. A fan-like rain of flashes revealed the machine gunner in the lead, and the shot sprayed Jim's plane in half a dozen places. She shivered under the attack, then the boy shut off the motor and let her slide into a tail spin. For a second she hovered uncertainly, then began to bob and bow this way and that, but soon she was whirling downward like a falling leaf. The wind over the desert was strong, holding her up, but she cut through.

As they made the perilous descent in rings,

Austin caught glimpses of the three pilots watching. He ducked his head forward as if he was at least badly wounded, and he pulled Mrs. Gonzalas into a limp heap. His eyes, or one of them was on the control board, and his apparently lifeless hand close to the instruments. The stick was between his knees and his heel was on the rudder-bar ready to get into instant action before they really took a header into the ground, and he prayed fervently that the men in the rear cock-pit were also "playing dead," or behaving becomingly for the occasion. Perhaps the enemy would think their task was accomplished and rush off toward Amy-Ran. As Arto had been an aviator in the war he would probably understand the present maneuver and not only play his own part, but coach his brother. The pointer on the altimeter spun around, one hundred feet, another, one hundred and fifty. They were going more quickly.

In the silence of their own machine, the motors of the others could be heard distinctly, and Jim's heart skipped a beat as one of them turned about and rushed off. It was evident that he at least was satisfied that they had downed their prey and he wasn't wasting time on postmortems. If the others, particularly the one carrying the machine gun would only take things as easily! He flipped the machine on her back and into as long a glide as possible, which wasn't at all unnatural. Every airman had seen planes act that way; as if they hesitated and hovered hoping to escape the inevitable crash. From that inverted position the boy could have shouted with joy as he saw the second machine turn swiftly and roar off toward the mountains. He too was convinced that the work was finished and he was heading for the fastness as hard as he could go. But the third plane, although it was circling against the sky toward the rocks and away from the scene of the smash-up did not pass over the rim. The altimeter sent its needle around in warning circles; they could not fall much further, but on they went. They were only five hundred feet from the ground and Jim tipped a bit for fear the position would injure Mrs. Gonzalas, whose face was flushed with the blood that had rushed to her head.

"Stand it a bit longer?" he asked.

"Si," she answered bravely, but he didn't require her to endure the strain more than a moment. They had passed beyond the rim of a low fold of sand hills, and there the boy felt sure that it would be safe for him to come to. Even against the white sand, the aviator, whose motor was racing, could not possibly distinguish from that distance what they were doing, so he righted the machine, let her glide on, and to his great joy he saw they would land on the hillside and that would slide them further. The wheels struck a smooth, hard surface, for which the boy was mighty thankful. It meant they hadn't landed in one of the dreaded cactus beds, also that they wouldn't sink into the ground. He could hear the machine getting further away, its engines waking the echoes, so he gave his own plane the gun to keep it from running into unseen danger.

The wide desert stretched before them, with its dark patches of shadows undefined in the moonlight. He couldn't tell whether they were rocks, dunes, or plants, but wisdom urged him to get above them quickly and he lost no time. Flying close to the ground, his eyes straining for threatening obstacles, they raced forward. Occasionally he glanced back toward the rim of the mountains but saw no one in pursuit. He was too low to choke off his engine even for a moment, then Arto spoke into his ear.

"We will observe for their return."

"Thanks. All right back there?"

"Much right. You are a great flyer. The marvelous Col. Lindbergh, he comes from

America, he would say you are the gooseberries."

"Aw," Jim chuckled, "I'm a ham flyer beside Lindy."

"At least we have gained some distance on them. Mrs. Gonzalas is—"

"Let her speak for herself," Jim handed over the tube and had to smile at the words, mostly Spanish but sprinkled with English slang and correct phrases, which tumbled from her lips. It was evident that she was telling them of her safety and also letting them know that she was getting a real kick out of the adventure. At last the conversation was cut off, and she settled into her seat comfortably prepared to enjoy the remainder of the trip. Jim guessed that the brothers had done their best to assure her that danger was passed. The miles were shooting behind them when suddenly something rose sharply ahead, so with nose in the air they zoomed for altitude, climbing a thousand feet. He did not glance back again for he knew they would soon pass beyond the desert stretch and have to ride high over another spur of the Andes. It had been hot in the valley, but now as they rose it was getting cooler, and his chart showed they were coming to the last but highest and widest folds of the range and he must be on the alert. He hoped that they had eluded the gang, but he wouldn't be too sure until they were safely on the ground with friends around them. Again he thought of the possibility that Cardow might learn of their escape, and have one or a dozen men waiting to pick him up before he could reach Cuzco.

Over the mountain range the clouds were forming, some in thick patches which settled low, like crowns around the rugged peaks, and Jim hoped that he could stay above the gathering mist until they were beyond the dangerous section. Thinking it over, he wondered if he had not been foolish to leave the desert. The plane carried a bottle of water so they would not have suffered from thirst for a few hours, and in the early morning he could have hopped off safely, seen the whole world, and the risk of being rediscovered by any of the gang would have been greatly lessened. They roared along between the moon and the thickening mist, and ahead banks of clouds were forming in dark masses as if preparing for a storm. Austin still planned to get a message to the laboratory men regarding the plan of Cardow to blow up the great rocks, although it did not seem likely that Ynilea or some of the observers constantly on watch could have missed seeing the outlaw men at work regardless of how carefully they were setting the dynamite.

If Mrs. Gonzalas had not been along, the Flying Buddy would have suggested to the brothers that they accompany him to the fastness, or wait for him at some plantation. Jim was rather glad that he was not a transportation pilot carrying women and children as well as men and freight from point to point. With just men and luggage a chap could take a lot of chances, but women had to be looked after so that no harm befell them. Tonight he had done any number of mighty risky things, but he had no choice. It was a case of do what he could and do it quickly in order to get away from the vicious brutes or be pumped full of lead.

"I think I hear a plane," Arto told him and Jim nearly jumped out of his skin. Quickly he shut off the motor, and sure enough, not far behind him, and a bit higher, was another plane. There was no mistake.

It sent out a long penetrating ray of light and if the pilot had not already picked them up, he would in a very few minutes.

"They come for us again?" Mrs. Gonzalas sat up quickly.

"Reckon so," Jim answered. He zoomed up with a roar, for he dared not dive into the protection of the thick mist and fly blind because if his altimeter went wrong even slightly, they would dash themselves against one of the hundreds of steep cliffs that stood out like giant walls.

"How do they know?"

"Perhaps one was sent to that place in the desert we were supposed to make a landing to see if we were alive and they discovered the trick; or some one may have located us later and given them word by radio. I don't know how they managed it."

"I see only one plane," she said hopefully. He glanced back.

"That will be less trouble than three. He tried to grin, but the effort was not highly successful.

"They gain," Arto spoke in his ear.

"How many?" Jim thought the plural pronoun must surely mean more than one machine.

"One only. It has guns."

"It is better that we did not stay in the desert," Mrs. Gonzalas remarked, and then he knew that she too had thought of that possibility.

"Reckon it is," he nodded.

"I will pray to the Mother of God. She deserts not the men on the sea and the men in danger," she spoke earnestly, and Jim was glad that she could do that. It would make her feel better. He did it himself many times. Not always when he was in danger. As he thought of it he couldn't recall ever praying when things were going wrong, but when they were flying over some magnificent scene, when he learned some new marvel of the universe, or when Bob got over being sick, then he had a feeling as if God was very close. There was a sort of smiling somewhere deep in him. He never tried to define it any other way; but it suited his purpose, and now, just thinking about it brought a quiet confidence to his mind and a steadiness to his body.

"He gains fast."

Jim glanced up and saw that the plane which was chasing them was not one of those that had turned back. Probably a more powerful one had been sent out with orders to bring them down and be sure of it. He took an instant to read his dials, glanced at the chart and calculated they must be nearing a valley, but no settlements were marked on it. The huge machine thundered gaining quickly until finally it was swooping almost onto them. Austin tried to dive out of its way, but this man did not let him get away with that trick, so he had to pull up. He tried a loop but came around near the other fellow, and then above the din of their motors came the steady spit of bullets, the streaks of flame, and it seemed as if the plane was hit in a dozen places at once. More shots racked her from propeller to tail. A bullet cut across the control board splintering the glass plates. Others ripped holes in the fuselage, and more poured through the wings. The plane lunged and rocked in spite of all the boy could do, and as he kicked the rudder-bar he realized that it was out of commission. Then the shots spit back and forth again, and a moment later the tank had been struck. Almost instantly it lighted and the blaze whirled about the machine.

"Get out of your safety strap," he shouted to Mrs. Gonzalas.

"I am," she told him in a moment. His own was loose, but he kept his seat while the machine, absolutely out of control, started down, nose first.

"Stand up," he called to her and helped her to her feet. "We want to stay with this as long as we can." He glanced at the altimeter, and after a moment, shouted: "I'll hold you by the strap. Don't pull the rip-ring until I tell you." By that time the plane was like a blazing rocket returning to earth.

"I am ready," she shouted in his ear.

"We want to jump as far as we can." He glanced about and saw the brothers poised above the rear cock-pit, standing close together. They were on the side opposite the enemy machine, which had to keep its distance for the moment. "Now, come!" The plane was tipping and they dropped off into space.

Jim could feel Mrs. Gonzalas clutch his belt strap and twist convulsively, then she gave a little scream. "Mio," The brothers had waited an instant longer, then they too slipped into space, sprawling like frogs, but Arto seemed to be close to Pedro and shouting encouragement to his brother. Down they dropped straight, while the air carried the machine away from them toward its destroyer.

"Don't wish you any extra hard luck, old timer, but I hope she makes you join this coming-down party."

"Mother of God—"

"Now pull the ring," Jim called, and she did. In a moment the great umbrella mushroomed out wide and Mrs. Gonzalas was dangling in safety. She glanced about in surprise at the ease of her descent, and then began to look for her husband.

"Mio," he called softly. It was more by intuition than hearing that she located the caller for above them the destroyer was circling as close as it dared.

Jim wished that the parachutes had dark

instead of light covers whose course could be followed through the night. He gave his undivided attention to his companion, and showed her how to catch hold of the ropes in order to spill air and direct her progress. She carefully followed his instructions, and at last they began to settle below the mist. Austin wasn't sure that he had been over the valley when they jumped, and he strained to see what was below them. At first he could make out nothing but rolling mist, then, to one side, he caught a glimpse of fire, like a camp fire in the woods and he prayed that they were not coming down into a pack of the enemies.

IX

TAKEN FOR A RIDE

As they descended suspended like some kind of Christmas ornaments from the huge parachutes Austin had to keep on the alert that his companion came through the experience safely, but his mind was busy with various other matters as well. He could hear the plane that had set their own on fire circling above them and while he realized that for a time its pilot was forced to keep his distance he knew the man could have easily punctured their parachutes and riddled their bodies with bullets, but he did nothing of the sort, which did not seem in keeping with his former vicious determination to get them out of the sky. This was puzzling and something to be considered soberly.

The De Castro's plane had shot down, buried its nose in the earth, and blazed so furiously for a moment that it lighted the vicinity in spite of the fog. Austin spilled air and saw that Mrs. Gonzalas did likewise so they would not land on the burning mass.

They drifted past it, saw the brothers just a bit lower, and vague shapes wavered toward them, like arms reaching up. On the opposite side of the ruined airship was the bon-fire, but although Jim strained his ears to hear, not a voice reached him. He thought it might be possible that the campers were asleep, but that seemed hardly probable for surely the fusillade of shots above the valley must have been startling enough to have aroused the most sound sleeper.

The fact that there was no sign of activity added to the boy's anxiety. Surely if it were merely a coincidence that they were dropping on someone's camp, that someone would be moving about in an effort to fathom the mystery of a battle in the air. Just then they began to settle below a grove of trees and Jim, whose eyes were on the ground, sent their bodies a few feet further to escape branches. In a moment they would be on their feet, and they were.

"That was fine. I saw a fire, so we are fortunate to have fallen near someone," Mrs. Gonzalas said happily. Just then her husband succeeded in releasing himself from the chute and rushing to her closed her in a warm embrace.

"Mio, you are safe," he choked, while his

brother thoughtfully undid straps for the woman.

"That fire, we will investigate," Arto suggested.

"With guns out," Jim answered. "It seems queer to me that we were not fired on in the air and we were driven down right here."

"Even so." Arto had not thought of that and his gun came out.

"Got many cartridges—"

"You ain't needin' em," a man's voice drawled so close that the four turned quickly, but it was so dark they could barely see the white blur of his face. It seemed to the castaways that he was not alone and this was immediately verified.

"Touchin' little scene of home," said a second voice. "Sort of too bad not to let em finish their love-making."

"Had to interrupt when they began to talk gats."

"You guys best be reaching kinda high so your hands won't get you into no trouble," he ordered, and the three men raised their arms, while one of their captors relieved them of weapons, wallets, and shells. When that was finished, the first one gathered the things together.

"I'm waiting fer you, General," he remarked.

"We'll march 'em to the welcomin' fire till we get the signal, Admiral," the "General" answered, and the procession started over a rough way toward the spot they had seen through the mist.

"Guess you was never in such good company before," the Admiral informed them. "Step easy here, cause there's a ditch, lady."

Wearily Jim fell in between the Gonzalas brothers, while the leader of the reception committee gallantly assisted the woman, who went forward with set face. Once a sob escaped her, but it was a small one, and she bravely controlled herself. Most women would have cried after such a heart-breaking series of disappointments. Presently they reached a large flat stone where the fire had been lighted and still blazed cheerfully.

"Right nice to have you folks drop in on us this way," the Admiral remarked sweetly. "Ain't no place in the world, no place where people are so neighborly as this here Peru."

"Have a cup of coffee, Ma'm. It'll warm you up plenty and the night's still young." He poured some of the steaming stuff into a tin cup and offered it to the woman, who accepted it promptly, for her teeth were beginning to chatter.

"The men, they too are cold," she pleaded.

"Sure, sure, there ain't nothin' mean about

us." Another cup was produced and the three men drank. It revived their spirits greatly, and the hot black mixture warmed them up.

"Thanks a lot," Jim said, then added, "What are you fellows going to do with us? These people have nothing to do with me—"

"Aw, we didn't ask you no questions, did we?"

"We can't tell yet, but we'll know before long," the General added.

"There it goes now—" They listened, then heard a series of distant shots, evidently from a small gun, spelling out some sort of code. It was none Jim recognized, but the men made notes on pieces of paper, and finally, when there was a pause, the general picked up a rifle which was near at hand, and fired three shots. A moment later the sound of the motor, which had been silenced during the exchange, boomed out again, and Austin knew that the machine gunner was on his way.

"Well now, ain't that nice." The men had their heads bowed over what they had written.

"You're wanting to know what we're going to do with you." The General looked at Austin and leered. "Well, Buddy, we're taking you for a ride." Jim caught his breath sharply for he had read that among gangsters being taken for "a ride" meant nothing more than being killed.

"But these people have done—"

"Aw, you gotta suspicious nature, Buddy. We're taking you for a real ride, in an aryplane."

"Them's the boss' orders." You kin rest yourselves ten minutes, then we're startin'," the Admiral volunteered, and the Flying Buddy gave a relieved sigh. They were probably being taken to the "Boss" whoever and whatever he was, and while there was no telling what fate had in store for them later, at least they were in no immediate danger of being bumped off.

"We ain't tyin' you up, or nuthin' like that, but we're tellin' you that these here woods is got a lot of Peruvian tigers scattered round in 'em and they ain't tame cats. That's only case you get a notion to do any runnin'."

"Thanks," Jim grinned. At least the pair did not appear to be so blood-thirsty as other members of the gang he had encountered, and this was something to be mighty grateful for.

The next few minutes were devoted to packing a roll of equipment into a pair of blankets, and with an eye to some possible future need, the General added the four chutes to the rest of the stuff. What food was left from their own meal was pressed on the prisoners, who ate it gratefully, especially Jim who felt as hollow as a gun barrel. At last they were ready to start, the fire was stamped out and the charred coals scattered, but as he stood waiting, the boy noticed a white mark on one of the nearest trees. The Admiral had a small flash light which he used to see that nothing was left behind, then taking a larger one from his pocket, he started around the rock.

"Ladies first," he nodded to Mrs. Gonzalas, who obediently fell in after the man. Jim came next, then the brothers, and the general brought up the rear.

Both the guards had their guns in hand, and a roll slung over their shoulders, but it wasn't fastened in any way, so Jim decided they were not going very far. Probably to some nearby open space where the plane, or planes were waiting. If there was only one it would have to be pretty large to carry them all, and the boy wondered, as they proceeded through the black forest, if the machine or machines were the ones that had been used to chase him earlier that night. He thought it must be long after twelve o'clock, but he realized that things had happened in swift succession and had not consumed as many hours as they seemed to. The flashlight, one in front and the other behind, made weird shadows of their movements and cut a sharp trail through the woods. In five minutes they reached the foot of a cliff, and the Admiral made his way straight to a narrow trail which reminded Austin of cattle trails in Texas, and they began to climb. Soon they were on a stretch of table land, and from somewhere came the dismal howl of a coyote.

"Oh," Mrs. Gonzalas shivered as the cry was taken up by other beasts, and she edged nearer to the men.

"You needn't be afeard, lady, not of the noisy ones. Tigers and them other cats don't make a sound, but if you see one watching you, then you got cause to shiver." The Admiral threw the light of his flash around cautiously and soon Jim saw the wheels of a large plane. It did not look like any of those that had taken part in the attack, but he couldn't be sure. As they drew closer he did not see any sign of a machine gun or a pilot, so he guessed that their captors were airmen.

"All aboard," the General ordered softly, and presently they were in the small cabin of what looked like a transportation machine. There was plenty of room for the six of them, besides two extra seats. Behind the passenger section was a compartment evidently meant for baggage and into this the rolls were tossed carelessly.

"Show your tickets," the Admiral invited quite as if he was conducting a party of tourists, instead of taking the group decidedly against their will to parts unknown. Jim thought of inquiring what their destination was to be, but changed his mind because he could hardly expect to be given an honest answer.

The Admiral took the pilot's seat, while the General perched watchfully in the rear so that any move made by one of the prisoners could be instantly observed and stopped. His rifle stood near at hand and a business-like six-gun was in his belt. There was the usual "trying," then the huge plane moved through the darkness, and as soon as its wheel lifted, all but a very small light was switched off in the cabin.

"You been real peaceful up to now," the Admiral reminded them, "En here's hoping your good judgment don't lead you astray while we're flyin'. There ain't no tigers, but the guns is fer use, pronto." He turned his attention to his job, and soon they were roaring through space.

The plane seemed to climb steeply, then curve, and Austin wished that his place was not in the center. If he could get a glimpse of the control board he could calculate something about the direction they were taking. Thinking about the huge plane he realized that with little light people on the ground would not observe that it was a big one, and unless there were other lights on the tail or underneath, the dim glow would make it appear as if it were a small machine. It seemed to the Flying Buddy as if they were making very good speed, and in a few minutes they were tearing along in a thick mist. They climbed again, and once they rushed into a storm. The wind blew furiously and rain beat on the fuselage. Mrs. Gonzalas, who was seated close to her husband, sunk her head wearily on his shoulder, and was soon asleep.

It was a mighty good thing that she could sleep, Jim thought. He would have liked taking a nap himself but he felt that he had to keep wide awake for an opportunity to escape might present itself and they would want to grab it while the grabbing was good. He could see Arto huddled low in his coat collar and although the man looked as if he were dozing, the boy was positive that the former aviator was doing nothing of the kind. He too would be alert for a slip on the part of their captors which would change their present position, making the captors the captives. A flash of lightning cut through the blackness and then Austin was not sorry that he did not have the place at the controls as they tore through the storm. The plane climbed heavily and leveled off above the rain, then shot forward at an amazing speed.

The Flying Buddy made up his mind that this was no ordinary plane but a specially built machine with extra engine power. Probably it was the property of one of the chiefs of the gang, perhaps the leader or Boss himself, but glancing about, Jim changed his mind on that last score, for the Boss would be sure to have his personal machine more luxuriously furnished, with curtains, cushions, and shiny trimmings. He had no idea why he thought the Boss would do that but he had never read of a leader of gangdom who didn't have a great deal of show and super-comfort in his surroundings. Once he closed his eyes, he couldn't help it, and as he dozed he thought that the General in the rear was creeping up on them with a glistening knife, but when his eyes popped open he saw that his imagination was playing tricks on him, for the guard was exactly where he had taken his place at the start.

As well as the boy could tell they had traveled nearly half an hour when the speed was decreased somewhat, and then he realized they were circling in wide loops. Perhaps they had reached their destination, and a few minutes later he was sure they had, for the motor was throttled and the plane began to glide. They had either passed through the storm, or it was over, for there was no sign of it. Glancing through the nearest window he noticed that they were descending in what looked like a rugged section of the country. They must be in one of the spurs of the Andes. He thought he glimpsed something that might be a lake, then he could see nothing more and decided that they were coming down close to the earth and on both sides of them were steep wall-like cliffs.

Jim yawned and stretched high in his seat trying to get a look at the control board, but the Admiral, in making the landing, completely obscured it from his sight. Arto too indulged in a prodigious fit of deep breathing but he was no luckier than Austin in reading their location.

"You can all wake up," the General informed them.

"Mio," Pedro called to his wife, who opened her eyes, stared about her in amazement, then glanced at her husband. Her eyes filled with tears and she buried her face against his breast and began sobbing bitterly.

"Aw, come now, lady, that ain't getting you no place," the General protested.

"Better keep off the water-works," the Admiral advised sharply.

"Be brave, querida mia," Pedro whispered trying to comfort her, but she continued to cry as if she were going to have a spell of hysterics.

"Can that," the General snapped. Pedro urged softly and in a few minutes the sobbing ceased. She dabbed her face with her handkerchief, and straightened her clothes.

"Mother of God," she prayed tearfully.

"Listen, Bo, make her quit that or I'll—give her something to pray over," the General snarled and his fingers clutched his gun aggressively. If he thought to frighten Mrs. Gonzalas into silence he used the wrong tactics, for she shrieked out wildly, crying harder than ever.

"You would—" Arto flared.

"I say," Jim interposed. "What do you want to scare her out of her wits for? No wonder she cried; waking up and seeing you."

"You kin save your compliments—"

"If you want her to stop crying, stop doing things to make her," Jim snapped angrily. "You're a big coward." He turned to Mrs. Gonzalas. "Don't you be afraid of him, or any of them, don't let them throw a scare into you now! You just grin and pretty soon things won't seem half so bad." Jim didn't like to see a woman cry, or a girl—anyone for that matter and he was mighty earnest about wanting Mrs. Gonzalas to dry her tears. He was standing beside her, and Pedro looked up at him with deep appreciation in his eyes.

"You are good—see Mio—Senor Jim Austin. In his land, the big Texas, he busts cows and broncs—wears a big hat to hold his head, and throws a rope so well Senor Bill Rogers goes out of business."

"Oh, blubbering whales—say—when you come to Texas I'll get Dad to show you how a lariat should be thrown," Jim interposed. At their united efforts, Mrs. Gonzalas looked from one to the other, blinked rapidly and although her hand trembled on her husband's arm, her lips parted in a smile. She controlled herself courageously, stifling the sobs, and out of the corner of his eye, Austin saw the guard step back as if satisfied that the prisoner would soon be comforted.

"In a large hat—big enough for your President—you look well," Arto helped, but his hand was gripped in his belt and by the pressure of his fingers on the buckle they knew that he longed for the minute when he could get them on the throats of the men responsible for their difficulties and his sister-in-law's suffering.

"Last stop," the Admiral bellowed.

"All out."

"Only they ain't leaving without some decorations." He produced clanking handcuffs. One pair he put on Pedro and his wife, and with the other he secured Jim and Arto together.

"Now you look more 'folksy'. Get a move on."

The manacles hampered them and as no more lights were turned on the four stumbled along the cabin to the low door. Jim lead the way, and had to stand on a brace while Arto came after him. Then the two jumped together, landing on something rather slippery, which Austin thought might be mossy stones. Pedro appeared almost immediately, for the Admiral was urging speed, so the two on the ground braced themselves to help. At last they were all out, and Jim glanced about him curiously. One thing he noticed, nothing seemed wet, so he decided that the storm had been a local and not a general one.

"You guys stay where you are," the Admiral snapped authoritatively.

"I got a gun on 'em."

They stood perfectly still a short distance from the plane, and Jim took a look at her.

The design was quite different from any he had ever seen; she was especially trim, and although he could not see well, he made up his mind that she was twin motored. If he got a chance to examine her more closely he would know something about flying her in case they could break away from their captors. There was no chance of doing anything of the kind now for the Admiral had them covered with a brace of six-guns, but just the same, Austin wasn't going to give up merely because of a pair of shooting irons.

X

SHIVERING ROCKS

"Hey you, come on en watch your step," the Admiral ordered abruptly although the little band of prisoners had seen or heard nothing which announced that the next move was to be made.

"Right-O, don't rush the mourners," Jim answered, then he turned to his bracelet-mate and grinned broadly. "After you, my dear Gonzalas."

"Pray, I beg of you go first," Arto responded equally cheerful.

"Now, none of your funny business," the General snapped suspiciously.

"Maybe you won't find things to laugh at—"

"We will as long as you're around, old comic strip," Jim told him, but he proceeded at the head of the awkward squad.

They seemed, as far as the boy could make out in the darkness, to be on a plateau, and he guessed it was somewhere in the coast range of the Andes. The spot on which they had landed looked like a great shelf, the outer edge of which must descend steeply. The wall they began to follow was high, made a long curve and appeared to be perpendicular. Once Arto stumbled, and in order to help them both, Jim's hand braced against the massive rock and he discovered that its surface was surprisingly smooth. That fact made the boy decide that they were above one of the numerous streams which had worn its way to its present depths through countless ages of rushing among the jagged cliffs until it had cut the solid foundation.

"Please, I slip," Mrs. Gonzalas said suddenly.

"I hold you," her husband assured her. The two ahead paused a moment to assist if they could.

"Come on, she can't slide off."

"Why can't you give us a bit of light?" Jim protested. He knew perfectly well that the ledge must be quite wide or it would never have been selected for a landing of the huge plane, but the woman couldn't reason things like that; she had no means of knowing.

"Aw, well," grumbled the General, but he went to the couple and proceeding beside them, using the smallest flash with its ray pointed directly on the route.

After that they made better progress for, although a chap may be perfectly positive that certain conditions must exist he will not fail to falter on his way if he cannot catch an assuring glimpse of where he is putting his feet. With seemingly endless piles of mountains mounting to the very heavens all about him, and knowing that perhaps only a few rods away the ledge drops off hundreds of feet, trying to walk forward in the darkness is a nerve-racking undertaking. Another thing that flashed through the boy's mind was that Gordon was exactly the type of enemy to order that they be taken to the ledge and shoved over out of his way forever. More than once he had been frustrated in his endeavor to rid himself of the Flying Buddies, and with each failure his hatred was growing. Sending the innocent Gonzalas over with his neighbor from Texas would not deter him for a moment. Arthur would reason that they knew too much and therefore were a menace to him.

"Turn in that cut," the admiral ordered.

They had reached a hall-like opening in the cliff, that looked as if it had been split out by highly clever stone workers, and here the General turned his flash, but he no longer held it close to the ground. It was likely that he did not fear its being seen so he was more liberal with the illumination. They had to go single file partly because of the narrowness of the way, and partly because of their manacled hands. They were all woefully tired and stumbling along with dragging feet. Jim began to wish that whatever the Boss had in store for them could be got over with immediately. He felt as if he simply couldn't go much further.

The hallway wound around, opened into a great cave-like tunnel, and just beyond that they came to a large square basin, like a great roofless room. Above one side the stones formed an arch which hid the occupants from sight of airmen and here Austin saw a fire, built well against the rocks; about it several men were stationed as if waiting. The arrival of the men with their captives did not create much excitement and Jim guessed that something of importance was about to happen, or someone was expected to arrive at any moment. The men were half lounging, their collars turned up and their caps pulled down, so at first he could distinguish none of them very clearly.

"Come over here," the Admiral ordered, and escorted his party some distance from the group.

"I'm going to sit down," Jim announced,

and promptly dropped to the ground, or rather the stones. "Whew, that feels better." He noticed some of the men glance indifferently in his direction, but the four of them made themselves as comfortable as possible while the Admiral and his companion stood over them, guns in hand.

Several minutes passed during which time no one spoke and as Austin leaned back to rest he looked up toward the sky, which was a clear cold blue with stars that seemed to have retreated to their greatest distance from the globe as if they rather disapproved of the actions of men. "Queer how different they look when we are flying near to them," he thought. "As if they are interested and want to be encouraging." He reasoned that the place they were in was probably near the coast and considerably north of Cuzco where the range of the mountains was broader, with wide stretches of uninhabited territory. The Flying Buddy felt sure that only in such a place would the great Boss have a stronghold such as this, and it was evident that the men were familiar with the section; enough so that they had a landing site as well as the corner with its overhanging ledge.

"Suppose it's the Boss they are waiting for," the lad whispered to Arto who was seated beside him.

"Si," Arto answered.

"Perhaps he's got some kind of cave or something. Do you know anything about where we are?"

"No. It might be east, far from Cuzco."

"I was thinking north—"

"The Andes are vast," Arto reminded him, and Jim nodded. There was no telling where they were. All they knew was that the Boss had ordered that they be brought at once, and it was apparent that no harm was to be done any of them for the present.

"Must be that he wants to try and pump me," was Austin's mental decision, and he shut his lips grimly determined to keep them closed and retain the secret this hated gang leader was determined to discover, regardless of the cost in money or men. He glanced curiously about the dim place but it was so dark and shadowy that he could not even be sure now exactly where the narrow entrance was that had admitted them. He wished that he could go to sleep and he saw Pedro trying to coax his wife to get some rest, but she was terribly frightened and her great brown eyes were wide open as if their lids would never close again. Just at that moment there was a slight stir near the fire, and in a couple of seconds the boy saw three men move quickly across the dark space and into the rim of light. Their backs were to the prisoners, and after a few words were exchanged in undertones which could not be understood by the captives, two of the men turned slightly, and then Jim almost jumped out of his skin.

"It is Cardow," Arto whispered, scarcely above his breath.

"And the fellow Gordon," Jim added. His mind was busy, and then he recalled that the gang lieutenant had said that he expected to go to Amy-Ran fastness by midnight. Surely it was long past that, but Jim's wrist watch was under his shirt cuff where he kept it while he was flying because there was a clock among the instruments of the dial-board.

"Bad men! I regret for my brother—"

"Yes. Any idea what time it is?" Jim asked.

"Nearly two o'clock when we arrive. Perhaps a little after now, ten or fifteen minutes. The night is very long," he sighed.

In that case, Jim calculated, they couldn't be near the fastness unless something had gone wrong; there had been delay in setting off the dynamite. Perhaps Cardow and Gordon had just returned from the blowing-up of the enormous rocks intending to report their success to the Boss. He glanced toward the two faces but there certainly was no trace of rejoicing in the expressions the men wore. Cardow was calm enough, but Gordon and the other chap puffed furiously at cigarettes and acted as if they anticipated something not altogether pleasant. It might be that they were in for a grilling from the Boss and did not look forward to the interview with any great relish. Then Cardow said something, and one of the men came toward them, spoke a sharp word to the guards, who straightened quickly.

"Get up, all of you, and come on," the General ordered.

"And no funny stuff," added the Admiral in a growl.

"Right-O," Jim answered, as they got to their feet. They were lead close to the wall instead of straight across the space, and presently the four were standing in the glow of the fire, which cast fantastic shadows about their feet. Gordon and Cardow eyed them blackly.

"Looks like a shower," Jim informed them cheerfully.

"You'll think it's a harder storm than that," Gordon shot back at him.

"That will do, Arthur, I am conducting this questionnaire. Is this the boy you had tied up?"

"Yes, it is."

"That's all I want to know." He turned to Arto. "Who are you?"

"I am Arto Carlos de Gonzalas; this *gentleman* is my brother Pedro, and his wife," Arto presented his family as ceremoniously as his hand-cuffed wrist permitted.

"Which of you conceived the idea of going to that dry fork of the river to-day?" Cardow demanded.

"I—"

"The project was mine, senor," Pedro spoke up quickly.

"What were you doing there?"

"We did nothing, senor," Pedro answered simply.

"You didn't just happen there!" Cardow snarled. "What did you go for? I haven't a lot of time to waste, darn it, and if you don't tell the truth, I'll have the boys stick your wife's feet in the fire—"

"Oh—" Mrs. Gonzalas started to scream, but a hand was put quickly over her mouth.

"Hush, mio," her husband begged earnestly, then turning to the Admiral who had silenced her, he snapped furiously, "You keep your hands to yourself, senor—"

"Let her alone," Cardow ordered, then he added to Pedro, "No one is going to hurt her if you tell the truth."

"I searched for platinum," Pedro told

them. "That is the truth, absolutely," and when he said it the men drew closer, eagerly.

"How did you happen to go there in search of it? Did you find any around that section?" Cardow questioned sharply.

"Si, senor, I did. Once, many weeks ago when hunting I got lost and wandered much time before I happen to cross the stream with the many branches and the dry fork. I found platinum. I noted the place, followed the stream and made my way out. Today—if it is to-day, I and my brother and my wife desired to return and get some of the mineral. We persuaded Senor Austin to take us in his airplane and he did. Before we start, we did not tell him our purpose in going," Pedro explained at length and deliberately. The men were crowding around now, and Cardow snapped a dozen questions, all of which the elder Gonzalas answered quite frankly.

"You did not find the stuff?"

"No, senor, we did not. The dry fork with the platinum I do not find, as you know."

"And you are positive that it was along a dry fork of that particular stream?"

"Positive! Why I did not find it—if I make the mistake—I cannot answer. Other planes came and we give up the search."

"Did you take any of it away with you

when you left the first time?" Gordon put in this question.

"Yes. At Panama I sold what I had. It was pure—excellent quality."

At that the men exchanged significant glances and then Jim was able to pick out Joe, Brick and Carp who had arrived at the dry fork with Cardow. He thought that some of the other men looked like those who had been in the gang that had tied the Flying Buddies and the two De Castros when the "volcano" had intervened to save them.

"Do you know anything more about the place?" Cardow turned to Arto.

"No."

"Did you ever go there?"

"No, I did not."

"Maybe while his brother was in Panama he went and cleaned out the bed," Brick suggested.

"Sure—that's what happened—what did you do with it?" Joe poked his face into the former aviator's.

"With my brother I went to Panama, and while we were there the notes of my brother were in the strong room at the bank in Lima," he answered coldly.

"Ah—"

"If I need any help from you fellows, I'll let you know," Cardow told them hotly.

"Now get back." They slouched to the wall and stared sullenly at the chief.

It suddenly occurred to Jim that if one of them ever came upon his lieutenant when the man was off guard, he would be knifed. As the boy got a better look at them they appeared to him more like a lot of hired thugs picked up from the numerous big cities in the northern continent, than men who were members of a well organized gang banded together under their Boss for the purpose of rediscovering the ancient secrets of the Yncas buried hundreds of years ago when their oppressors were annihilating them by the thousands and stealing their vast treasure.

"That is all there is to tell," Pedro spoke up quietly.

"Have you any idea how you happened to make a mistake about the place?" Cardow asked, but although he was inquiring into something which was really none of his business, there was nothing offensive in his manner.

"I have not," Pedro answered, then added, "The rest of the day we have been—our minds otherwise occupied."

"You have had rather a hot time of it. Why on earth did you run away? I saw the plane before we came down and we found tracks among the rocks, but you had vamoosed. What did you do that for?"

"My wife should be protected. The first plane came, there was a fight—a man was killed—"

"Yes—just a minute, Cardow—you saw that—now how did the fellow Alonzo get killed?" Gordon demanded.

"The trapper was offensive—I believe he claimed that you two were what you call—double-crossing him. The other man jump, very mad, and the hunter threw the knife. He went down at once—a woodsman's aim is always excellent," Pedro explained, but they wished that Gordon could have been implicated in the murder of Alonzo.

"Well, that ought to satisfy you," Gordon snapped at Joe. Although the fellow made no comment his face was ugly.

"Every darn thing that you've been in has been shot to blazes," Brick flared. "Tain't no wonder we're kinda tired of you."

"That will do," Cardow ordered. He started to turn to Jim, but just then a man hurried toward them.

"He's back, Cardow, with more stuff, and putting it under."

"It better work this time, or blast his hide, he'll get some blasting! We're not hanging around here all night!"

"He say's it will be set in a few minutes."

"All right, come back and tell us when he's ready." Austin heard this exchange, and then he made up his mind that they really were near Amy-Ran fastness. The gang must have tried to blow up the stones, but something had gone wrong with the explosives.

"All right." The fellow started away, and Cardow called him.

"Tell him to put it well around that low shelf—"

"That's what he was doing when I left."

"Very well. That's the rock that tipped and scared the wits out of the bunch, so that's one place we can be pretty sure is worth getting under. And warn him to have the charges so the whole works will not blow everything inside to thunder. That stone is hollow as a drum, I know, and I'll have no more of those half baked jobs. The Boss will be along himself, and if things aren't working right—" He didn't finish the sentence and at the announcement that the "Boss" was expected, the men took on a more alert attitude.

"Yes, he knows, but I'll remind him again." The chap hurried off so quietly there wasn't even one step heard, and almost immediately he had disappeared.

Jim wondered how soon the great leader would appear, and he also wondered if the Peruvian police chief was aware that this "Boss" of gangdom was in his country. Recalling the man with the Green Mask who had taken charge of things the night on the ledge, Austin expected that the real head of the vast organization would probably appear in some similar disguise. It was a pretty theatrical sort of get-up, but the lad decided that the Boss did not dare permit any of his men to know him personally, for no doubt every disgruntled one would betray him to the police if he got a chance.

Cardow turned toward him again, but before a question could be put, Gordon spoke in a low tone to the lieutenant. When the discourse was finished, the leader nodded impatiently.

"Now, look here," he snapped. "I'm not wasting a minute on you. We know that you are in with the bunch we are after, so, you answer my questions, everyone of them, and no stalling."

"I'll answer anything I can," Jim promised.

"See that you do."

"First, come across with what you know about the Haurea's and what they are doing. Where are they located?"

"The Don has a large ranch which adjoins my father's in Texas,"

"We know he has a ranch there—now, no stalling—I told you before. If you don't come out with the truth, I'm going to burn the whole bunch of you right here until you loosen up—see—"

"Yes, I see." Jim's face paled and his eyes rested a moment on the Gonzalas. He had no doubt that Cardow would carry out his threat and the woman would receive no kindlier treatment than the men, but he bit his lip and clenched his fists. Arto's fingers closed reassuringly over his own. Then another figure ran through the opening toward the fire and everyone turned to see him.

"Did you get him?" Gordon snapped.

"We got him—"

"Where is he?"

"Cooked!"

"Cooked? What do you mean?"

"Just what I said. We followed the plane all afternoon, brought it down ablaze, and the Caldwell kid went up with it; ain't that plain enough?"

XI

TREASURE

"That's a good job done," Gordon declared viciously.

"How do you get that way?" Cardow snapped furiously. Then he turned to the messenger. "You were told that the boy was to be brought in, weren't you?"

"Yes we were, Cardow, but we couldn't make it, I tell you."

"What the blazes happened?"

"We picked him up in the middle of the afternoon as he was headin' for the De Castro's. He didn't pay much attention to us, waggled his wings a couple o' times, and played around like he was feelin' good. That plane of his is the fastest thing in the air, I'm tellin' you, and we had a hard time to catch up with him; only did it when he slackened in the fog; then we got on all sides of him and when he came out we were ready. Gave him the lead as fast as we could pour it out. The machine blazed up like a paper lantern and turned into a tail spin."

"How high were you when you made the attack?"

"High enough. Nearly thirty thousand feet."

"Did he use his chute?"

"No, he didn't. We kept close coming down with him and we could see him foolin' round, like he was trying to get control again and put the fire out. He acted like he didn't notice how fast he was shootin' till he almost hit."

"Yes—well?"

"We were right with him to pick him up if he was alive, but he landed on a farmer's hay stack; it must have been dry as powder, for the whole thing went up in smoke in less than five minutes. I'm telling you the truth. We couldn't get him out and he didn't use his chute." The fellow's jaw protruded, and then two other men came toward the light.

"He's givin' you the goods straight, Cardow. We carried out orders exactly like we were told, and if the kid had jumped, we'd have got him safe, but he didn't and that's that."

During this recital Jim frowned in puzzled wonder, and even though the first man had said "Caldwell," the boy did not immediately grasp the fact that it was Bob, his Flying Buddy they were discussing, then, it went over him as if someone had given him a powerful blow that shook his whole body. Queer flashes of light shot through his brain and before his eyes. His throat seemed to swell until he felt as if he were being strangled, while a cold clammy perspiration oozed from every pore in his body, as he realized what they were saying. Bob was dead! Burned in a blazing plane that landed on a haystack! His body swayed, and then he was conscious that Arto's arm was supporting him.

"Get hold of yourself," the man whispered huskily. "You know the boy they got?"

"He's my brother—my step brother—my Buddy—"

"Easy—listen—perhaps it is a trick they have made up to scare you into talking of what you do not want to tell," Arto suggested.

"Perhaps it is—but I guess not—Oh!"

"Brace yourself, old man. Close we will watch and perhaps the morning will find us in changed positions. Be ready! I have found that for my wrist this hand-cuff is large. With it off, that will help. Keep close to my brother, so I can speak to him. When the time comes, these pigs shall pay—"

While this discourse was taking place, Cardow and Gordon were questioning the air-fighters, and at last they were convinced that no trick had been played; that young

Caldwell had not escaped from them. Gordon glanced maliciously toward Jim as if anxious to hear the same news of the second Flying Buddy. Cardow turned about and his eyes rested a moment on Austin, but before he could continue his interrogating, the man who had promised to report progress, came running to them.

"It's ready to shoot." At that the whole gang sprang forward, including the two guards, but Gordon stopped short.

"Don't let them out of your sight," he ordered brusquely to the Admiral and the General paused and returned to their charges, apparently none too pleased at the command.

The group waited tensely, Jim fiercely endeavoring to get his mind off the ghastly details of his Buddy's death as well as to keep from thinking how the terrible news would affect the boy's mother, and his own Dad. He could not help recalling the numberless times they had faced difficulties together and the seemingly limitless supply of side-splitting ejaculations that sprang to the younger boy's lips and never failed to bring a laugh which relieved the tension of deep feeling. Just then a series of noises were heard, a little like the regular popping of a rifle, and Jim guessed that it must be the explosions of the dynamite. He was surprised that the sounds were not greater and that he felt not the slightest quiver of the earth. This made him believe that they must be some distance from the Amy-Ran fastness.

"Come along. I ain't waitin' here," the Admiral urged, and the General acquiesced without hesitation.

"We can bring 'em with us and see what's doing. They can't get away no matter where we are," he argued. "March, you, en fast."

They started at once and this time had a fairly good light so they could easily see where they were going. Presently they were hurrying through the hallway, but they turned off before they were half way to the entrance near the plane. Five minutes they scrambled and then the route widened out and descended steeply by way of a gully that was paved with small stones which had probably been washed there during flood seasons and heavy rains. This brought them onto a sort of ledge where they stood suddenly in a good light that reflected a lower ledge about five rods away. Jim could see men hurriedly crowding on this other bit of table and then he was sure that it was the spot where he and the De Castros had been held prisoner.

"Come on, they've got something. I'm going over."

"March, and go fast."

The General and his fellow guard were determined to see what was taking place and not to be left out of anything, but their eagerness did not make them careless with their captives. They ran as fast as the damp moss permitted along a barely perceptible trail which wound several rods above the ledge on the other side of the canyon, and finally they made the crossing by leaping from great stones about which the water raced swiftly. Soon they too were on the ledge and then Austin saw, to his utter astonishment, that an enormous rock had been jarred out of its base, and behind its thick sagging wall, was some sort of cave, into which the men had leaped.

"Glory be, its the treasure," the Admiral gasped in awe as he stared about him.

"Look at them jewels—me pal, we're richer then Henry Ford en Rockeyfelley en the hull bunch."

The place they were in made Jim catch his breath with dismay for there was no mistaking it—no denying the fact that it was a treasure storage containing wealth untold. He judged that it was one of the "hiding houses" the Ynca Indians had secured for themselves to get away from their persecutors, to conceal their vast treasure, and worship the Sun as their ancestors had done for hundreds of years. In the middle of the furthest wall was a great sun of hammered gold and about its rim a wide band of precious stones so brilliant that they sparkled and flashed in the glare of the lights that Cardow and his men carried. In front of the sun was a high platform, and beneath that were wide seats made of stone. There were tall jars of pottery made in beautiful designs, inlaid with gold and emeralds.

Brick shinned up one of the large ones, stared into its wide mouth, then dipped in his hands. He brought them up dripping with jeweled ornaments of exquisite workmanship and brilliancy, then began to fill his pockets, but in his eagerness he failed to hang on, and came sliding swiftly to the stone floor, which was laid in colored squares with patterns that looked like historical pictures of long ago conquests. For a few minutes the men acted as if they thought they were asleep, but with Brick's find, they all fell upon the nearest object with guns and knives and began to hack off the treasure. Then suddenly a noise from outside startled them, and for an instant they paused, but when they soon saw that it was a deluge of rain coming down amid the crash of thunder they continued in their mad rush to get the treasure.

"Well, I got it open for you," one of men declared to Cardow.

"Sure you did. It's great work and good that this didn't get covered over. We'd have had some time digging it out. I'll tell the boss when he comes."

"I never tried to blast such rock, but by George, I tumbled the very best one down," the chap added with satisfaction.

"You'll get yours all right. We've been looking for years for this place and now we have it. We're set for life—all of us, and some to spare," Cardow answered. While he talked with him the men were behaving like a lot of fellows suddenly gone mad. Some of them sang, others rolled on the floor, more danced gleefully about marvelous furnishings, and many lolled on rich tapestry-covered couches. The place was beginning to look as if a cyclone had struck it, when Cardow turned furiously. "You fellows quit this, now, quick." He drew out his guns and flashed them from one man to another.

"Aw, gwan," one defied him. "We got what we come for."

"Sure. Take your share and close your trap. We been listenin' to you fer weeks, and we ain't taking no more sass." Several guns, whose butts were being used for hammers, were turned on the lieutenant, but he did not flinch.

"Listen, if you don't obey orders, how would you like to tackle the forests with your pockets full of gold and not a drop of water? You can't get out of this place without a plane."

"Aw, well, what do you want?"

"Just straighten this place up so the Boss can see it as it is, or was, see? He'll be madder than blazes if it's wrecked before he gets here," Cardow told them.

"All right. How long will it take him to come?" one demanded.

"Not more than half an hour, probably not that long. I'll send for him."

"That suits me."

"I'll go for him," Gordon volunteered. He was standing beside the huge stone that had been blown out of its place, and as he spoke, Jim noticed that the Texan seemed intensely interested in what he saw.

"Hurry along. Tell him what a find it is and that the men want to get to work cleaning it up as quickly as possible."

"I'll tell him."

"And tell him what a splendid piece of blasting it is. You might take some of these jewels." Cardow picked up a brimming handful which Gordon dropped into his pocket.

"I'll tell him all that, and some other things," Gordon answered.

"What do you mean, some other things?" Cardow demanded.

"I'll tellin' him this thing looks fishy to me—"

"Fishy, you're crazy—"

"Maybe I am crazy, but just the same, it's too easy." Without another word he walked out into the storm, and a few minutes later they heard the unmistakable roar of the engine as the machine raced through the sky. Joe strolled to the entrance and glanced out.

"Rotten night—"

"Tain't night no more, Buddy, it morning—"

"Well, it's blacker en pitch," Joe persisted. He walked about glancing from one treasure pile to another and occasionally running his hand over one of the giant ornaments.

"Got something on yer mind?" one of the men asked him.

"Yes. I'm wonderin' what in blazes Gordon's meanin'."

"Aw, he's just talkin' too much, like he always does," Brick volunteered.

"Sure, he's always doing that."

"I'm wonderin' if he'll queer the works—"

"Yer nuts. What kin he do? Look what we got—"

"I know, but I'm doin' some thinkin' by myself. Maybe he ain't bringing the Boss back at all, and we'll sit here waitin—"

"And not get nothin'?" snapped Joe.

"Might be sumpin like that—"

"Listen, Joe—if Gordon and the Boss are not here in half an hour, we'll divide this stuff up among ourselves and leave him what we can't carry away. I know he'll come and there's no funny business about it. You agree to that—"

"A lot kin happen in half an hour," Joe answered.

"Say, whose turning off the lights?" one of the men further back in the temple room demanded sharply.

"Nobody's turning em off."

"Reckon my battery's on the fritz." One chap examined his flash, then exclaimed in disgust, "Yes, the bloomin' blighter has gone dead on me."

For several minutes no one spoke and the four captives, who had been shoved into a corner, out of which they could not get without being seen, were listening and watching mutely. The Gonzalas, who probably knew nothing about the ancient history of Peru and its long line of magnificent rulers who had been wiped out of existence centuries ago, stared about them as if they thought they had been brought to some magic cave which was more wonderful than they had ever dreamed any spot in the world could be. Austin's thoughts were divided between sorrow over the destruction of his Flying Buddy, and regret that after all the generations of careful guarding of the secret, it should at last be discovered and so ruthlessly looted. He wondered how it happened that Ynilea or some of the Laboratory men had been unable to prevent the loss, and then he began to wonder anxiously if anything had happened to the great laboratory and its army of scientists.

"Jimminy Christmas, my light's going on the blink," Carp snarled.

"Ain't it near half an hour?" Joe demanded.

"It's only ten minutes," Cardow answered. His watch was lying on the smooth back of one of the seats, and most of the men were gathered close enough so they could see the minutes ticked off. A few of them sat patiently, while others strolled about, surreptitiously slipping small jeweled ornaments into their pockets. Five minutes more passed, and then one of the men started toward the opening, and in a moment he whirled sharply.

"Where's that door?" he yelled.

"The door?"

"Yeh, the way we got in," he snarled. As one man they rushed to his side and their jaws dropped.

"I knew it was some trick." Joe sprang at Cardow with a savage snarl and would have caught him by the throat if a gun had not been poked into his face.

"That will do!" He made his way toward the entrance. "What's the matter with the door?"

"It's closed," one shrieked with terror. "Closed tighter'n a tomb."

"Hey, listen men, you needn't be so frightened. Don't jam the thing and just as soon as Gordon gets back they'll open it easily from the outside; but be careful you don't fix it so they can't," Cardow urged, and a few of the men got somewhat over the panic.

"Ain't it most half an hour?" one asked anxiously.

"Twenty minutes. Ten minutes more and we'll be out. Now, don't lose your heads and queer the whole works." He spoke so coolly that some of his courage and common sense was caught by the others, and they grinned sheepishly at each other as they drew away from the door.

"I remember reading about them sailors canned up in that submarine—"

"Shut up—"

"Maybe Gordon closed that thing himself," another suggested.

"Say, will you crape-hangers keep still!" Cardow snapped, but his voice was neither as cool nor as steady as it had been. After that the place was so still that the ticking of the watch could be heard clearly, with an occasional sharp intake of breath as a man struggled to maintain control of himself.

"Put the wife back," Arto whispered to his brother. "They will not keep so calm." Quietly Pedro moved in front of the woman and Arto stepped close so that their bodies formed a barrier for her. For a moment Jim did not understand what they were doing, but when he realized that the Gonzalas expected some sort of mad scramble, he took a place as near as he could get. Then he was surprised to notice that the hand-cuff dangled from his wrist and that his cuff-mate had slipped out. Quickly the boy drew the empty ring up his sleeve and put out his hands as if they were still secured.

It seemed as if hours passed, and twice flash-lights dimmed, leaving the temple room in deeper darkness. One by one the men bent over the watch, checking off the minutes, and finally a group of them went to the great stone door that had made them prisoners. With ears pressed against the enormous block they listened for a sound from the world outside, but drew away when the lack of noise set their nerves on edge. Then one tapped sharply with the butt of his gun, waited an instant, but got no response. They tried this again but without success.

"It's half an hour," someone announced hoarsely.

"They're not coming—they're not, blast them!" Joe shrieked. He pounded his fists futilely against the immovable stone, and with that bedlam broke loose as the men screamed and hammered everything they could get their hands on against the unperturbed rock. In the melee the last light flickered, leaving them in a writhing, twisting mass of panic-stricken humans. Once or twice Cardow's voice rose above the din as he endeavored to restore quiet, but it was promptly drowned by the screams of the gang.

"Get further away," Arto urged. The captives moved cautiously along the wall until at last they were on the opposite side from where the entrance had been. From somewhere a faint light shone before the Sun-God, and Jim decided that it came from the clusters of brilliants set in the wide band. The men continued to fight and scream, but their voices were growing hoarser. Some were crying like infants, and this noise, Jim thought, was the most awful.

"The air," Pedro said softly.

"I'll feel for a crack," Arto suggested. "Hang on to me, Senor Jim." He dropped to his stomach, and Austin caught his trouser leg, then when Gonzalas moved further, the boy too lay flat, while Pedro clung to him, and Mrs. Gonzalas knelt beside her husband. She was praying quietly.

Across the temple the struggle was growing less furious, as if the men were becoming exhausted from their efforts or over-come by the closeness of their prison. For several minutes Arto wriggled close to the wall, his hands running lightly and swiftly over the space until at last he paused, they heard him take a deep breath, then he raised himself.

"Send her," he whispered. Pedro moved his wife forward and Arto made her lie on the floor, her face pressed against a tiny opening through which came a very thin streak of air from the outside world.

"I will not take it all," she declared.

"Stay there, mio," her husband ordered more firmly than Jim had heard him speak to her before, and she protested no more.

"We will find others," Arto assured her softly.

"Is she still cuffed to you? Jim asked.

"No. I took it off long ago," Pedro answered. "A man's cuff on a small woman—it was easy."

"My husband, permit me to share the hole with Senor Jim," she begged earnestly. "But for us he would not—"

"Never mind me," Jim whispered hastily, "I'm doing fine," but his head was already dropping forward on his breast. He tried to raise his hand to loosen his collar, but the effort was too great, and he closed his burning eyes with a weary sigh.

XII

GROSS EXAGGERATION

As the air grew more and more suffocating and the Flying Buddy slipped off into unconsciousness he had a hazy idea that someone was moving about him and that a queer hood, like the special gas mask the Don had given them when they started off in the "Lark" from Texas, was slipped over his head. When that was adjusted the pain in his throat eased and the lids of his eyes lost their sting. It seemed to Jim as if he remained in the great temple, which slowly grew lighter until each object stood out distinctly. Across the floor the members of the gang were huddled in a lifeless mass, but beside him, the bodies of the Gonzalas lay relaxed, as if they were asleep. There was no trace of suffering on any of their faces and he could see the woman breathing naturally.

It was a strange sort of experience and Austin wondered if he were dead. It made him think of a story he had once read, an odd tale of a man who was killed and he opened his eyes into a new world where he could see former companions and places. For a time the chap wandered like one lost, trying to communicate with his friends, but finally he saw a more beautiful land and hastened to enter it. But Jim decided that if he was dead his consciousness was entirely different from the author's fancy, for he could not move. However, there was no feeling of discomfort. He was perfectly content to rest and watch.

The Temple-room was quietly being restored to order, the upturned vases straightened, the things the members of the gang had used to hammer or pry off gold and jewels were gathered into a pile, and finally, when all was re-arranged, a weird figure made its way to the Gonzalas and Jim, who very much wanted to scream, but he couldn't, and after that he didn't know anything more.

When the boy opened his eyes some time later he was lying on a very comfortable couch on a cool terrace, and he blinked in the sunshine. Again he remembered the strange story of the man who had been killed, and then he was sure that he had died of suffocation in the temple room after the door had imprisoned them, for now he was in the midst of surroundings indescribably lovely. Some distance away he saw figures moving about, men, women, and children, and from behind him came the pure notes of a fine violin played by an artist. The music fitted into the scene and phrases of it harmonized perfectly with the gurgle of water running over stones and the hum of bees hovering above clover blossoms. He drew a deep breath of contentment but felt no desire to move or take a part in the leisurely activity.

From off in the sky he heard the roar of a motor as it carried one of the air-birds through the heavens, but Jim did not bother to turn his head. The notes of the violin blended now with the deep tones of the plane, and it seemed to the lad as if they even picked up the whistle of wind through the wires, only it was sweet as if the breeze played across the strings of a great harp. Altogether he thought that heaven was a most desirable state of consciousness and writers had never half done it justice. Idly he tried to think of appropriate sentences which would give earthlings a better idea of its charm and desirability, but they were elusive and trite as they formed in his mind, so he gave up.

Then suddenly he remembered that artists always gave heaven's residents wings, so he raised himself on his elbow to observe this phenomenal appendage, but if the nearest angel possessed the feathered means of locomotion, they were folded tightly and out of sight. This was a bit disappointing, and then Jim noticed that the particular individual he had under observation looked strangely familiar, and a moment later he recognized Mrs. Gonzalas, who was walking quite like a mortal about a marvelous garden. A young chap was striding beside her, and then Jim sat right up.

"Bob," he called. "Gee, I'm glad to see—" The two turned quickly at the sound of his voice and started toward him.

"Well bucking bullfrogs, did you come to at last?" Caldwell's smile went from ear to ear, in fact it was so wide that it went almost around his head. "I thought you were never going to." The Flying Buddy was beside his pal, but there was nothing unearthly about those features. Jim was on his feet, which wobbled uncertainly, and in a second Bob's arm was about him. "You take things easy for a bit, old timer and you'll be right as a trivet."

"I feel great," Austin declared—"Gee—I say, Bob—this is sort of queer, isn't it—I mean—" He looked at his pal uncertainly.

"It'll straighten out fine first thing you know, old timer—be hunky dorry—but take it easy," Bob insisted, and he pressed the older boy back to the couch. "Give yourself a few minutes—"

"Oh sure, I suppose so, but it's sort of odd getting adjusted—"

"Feel badly anywhere?" Bob asked. His tone was puzzled.

"No, no, I don't think so. I feel fine." The two sat quietly for a few minutes and then things began to appear less transparent. "I say—Bob—mind telling—"

"Telling what?" Bob wanted to know.

"Oh nothing, but—I say—it's sort of queer, isn't it? Dad and your mother, they'll be kind of shot to pieces, won't they?"

"They won't know anything about it," Bob answered quickly. "Not a word; that is, not for a while." This was a startling announcement, then Jim decided that for some reason or other the news of the Flying Buddys' disaster was to be kept from the family.

"I believe he still has a little fever," Mrs. Gonzalas remarked softly and then someone came, a glass was pressed to Jim's lips, and tender hands forced him to lie down on the couch. He closed his eyes again, intending to open them immediately, and he thought he did, but it was really hours later. This time he was in a real bed in a large comfortable room, and he saw someone bending over him.

"Oh, hello, Ynilea."

"Hello yourself and many of them. How do you feel?"

"Top hole, but gosh—I say I'm not dead, am I!"

"Not so that you can notice it," Ynilea answered. "You are very much alive, young man."

"Yes. Funny." Jim's face was sober. "I dreamed I waked up on a place like the Don's terraced gardens and Bob was there—my Buddy—" His lip quivered.

"Well, I was there, and I am here. I say—"

"Bob—" Jim sat right up. "You—are you alive?—"

"And how!" Bob chuckled cheerfully. "Now I know what you've been raving about, old man—"

"Then it was a trick of Cardow's or Gordon's?"

"No—but it was a trick. We'll tell you all about it as soon as you are stronger."

"I'm strong as an ox, but gosh, I'm empty as a tank."

"That is a detail which shall be attended to pronto," Ynilea spoke up, and it was. A tray, prepared with the greatest care, was brought in, and Austin was mighty glad to see it. His hand trembled a bit, but Bob helped him and by the time the meal was finished he felt like a new man.

"Now, tell me about that—why Bob, the fellow said they dropped you on a pile of hay and you were burned to a cinder. Now, what did happen?"

"The report of my demise, as the late Mr. Clemens put it so neatly, was greatly exaggerated, although I do not mind telling you, my esteemed brother, that my supposed bier was an imposing spectacle; quite remarkable and most enjoyable—that is as a spectator. As the principal character in the drama it might not have been quite such a treat."

"Well, for the love o'mike, tell me about it, and don't drag it out till doomsday," Jim urged.

"Delighted. You might be donning your pants while you listen, that is, if you feel equal to doing two things at once—"

"I'll tie the pants around your neck if you don't start."

"You recall that I brought the "Lark" to the Lab to have the new radio installed and to see the latest experiments in the horticultural laboratory. On the way up I happened to observe that I did not have the heavens all to myself. In fact, I shared them with two rather large planes that were decorated with right good-looking machine guns and ugly mugs behind them."

"Wow."

"Same here. Then, I couldn't shake the babies, and suddenly I realized that the "Lark" was flying all right, but she wasn't doing a blooming thing I told her to. Then I waked up to the fact that she was being managed from the lab. So I thumbed my nose to the high-command, and let her go. She came right home, like a good girl, leaving a stream of smoke in her trail and by way of the highest cloud bank."

"They lost you."

"They did. Then, of course the lab. men, inquisitive guys as you know, watched to see what my escort was about, and they thought up the lovely little scheme of having me start home when I was ready, go my carefree way, retire again to a cloud bank, and then return here to watch my demise. The bandits chased me, in the cloud they picked up another plane, with a charming dummy of myself at the controls, they filled the thing full of lead, and you know the rest. I got a big kick out of it. If you will pardon my mentioning it, it is customary to put both legs in your pants. They set better—"

"You brat—" Jim made a dive at his step-brother, who ducked with a broad grin.

then his face sobered. "You didn't have such an easy time of it, did you, old man?"

"It wasn't exactly a path of roses," Jim admitted. "The worst part was when the airmen came and said they had landed you."

"They did not let me in on it from the laboratory, but I've seen the records since," Bob said gravely. "Guess Ynilea was afraid that I could not stand the racket."

"Your guess is correct," Ynilea declared. "And how are you now, Jim? We owe you a vote of thanks for your part." Jim flushed.

"I say, ever heard the national anthem of Siam?" he inquired and Bob snorted, for he knew the answer.

"Perhaps I haven't. I'll bite, what is it?"

"O what an ass-I-am," Jim chanted. "I never thought of you helping, not once, but I was sort of surprised that you let them get the "Lark," and that dynamite stuff set. You know, I was scared all over for I thought something awful must have happened to you-all up here—that the Boss and his gang really got you."

"They didn't. We got many of them, or they got themselves, but we didn't get the Boss, as you call him."

"Gee, wish you'd let me have the dope," Jim urged.

"Surely. Of course we knew when they

were placing the charges, so we set a few charges of our own. We spoiled the first set for them, and Cardow sent for more. We spoiled that, but they did not know it. They heard a noise and the big stone rocked out of place revealing the treasure. That went to their heads and we hoped to have them all inside when the stone returned to its place, but Gordon got suspicious. When he told Cardow that he would tell the Boss it looked 'too easy' we were sure the big gun would not come and walk into the trap, so we sprung it without him or Gordon."

"Oh. But I say—"

"A couple of us went in and put masks on you and the Gonzalas, and the others—those who hadn't been killed in the struggle to get away, smothered."

"But gee, Gordon took a pocket full of jewels—"

"When he took them out to show them, they powdered in his hand. All that stuff was fake; arranged to make them ready to cut each others throats to get it," Ynilea explained.

"Jumping jelly fish, it surely looked like the mints of the world rolled into one," Jim declared.

"Didn't it! You remember I told you once

that if any of the gang discovered one of the strongholds they would get very little?"

"Sure!" Jim nodded, then he remembered the Gonzalas. "I thought I saw Mrs. Gonzalas here. You said that you put masks on them too—are they all right?"

"They are and they are leaving presently Like to see them off?"

"Sure. Jinks, they have had so many disappointments crowded into a couple of days," he said regretfully.

"Come along." The Sky Buddies followed arm in arm, and soon they entered a plain little apartment which looked exactly like hundreds of other homes of well to do families. There was no evidence of luxury, or anything especially marvelous, and Jim immediately guessed that the rooms were arranged for such an emergency; a time when guests could be in the real Amy-Ran fastness without actually seeing anything which would appear out of the ordinary. It was like the residents of persons of culture. When the boys and their escort entered, the three Gonzalas were just finishing luncheon, and they rose quickly at sight of Jim.

"You are safe and well," Mrs. Gonzalas' eyes filled with tears, but she blinked them back. "Into great trouble we got you."

"We rejoice that the fresh air which came

through the crack helped to keep you alive until these men got us out. The others are dead. It is a good thing. They are wicked," Pedro said earnestly, and Jim realized that the little family thought they understood how they happened to be saved.

"I prayed to the Mother of God and she helped us," Mrs. Gonzalas said softly.

"She surely did," Jim declared.

"We are leaving for home—"

"There is one question that I wanted to ask you," Ynilea interposed. "In your preparations for the search of the platinum did you spend all your savings?"

"Yes, and on the home we put a mortgage," Pedro admitted. "It was very foolish."

"Well, as I explained, much of the stuff that was in the ancient temple for so many years, crumbled as soon as the air got to it, but there are a few hard stones which had not deteriorated in the course of time. You have suffered greatly, and I should like to present them to Mrs. Gonzalas." He produced a small leather pouch and put it into her hand. She gave a startled gasp and stared at her husband.

"You have done too much for us—"

"*You* deserve the reward," Arto added quickly.

"It was a pleasure. I am a quiet man and

have plenty for the rest of my life. You have a little son. This will, I hope assist you to pay the mortgage and give him an education. Do keep it," Ynilea insisted, and he refused to take it back.

"Go ahead, take it, then you won't need to go off hunting again for platinum. There isn't much of it in these mountains anyway. I heard that on the best authority only a few days ago," said Jim.

"You are most good." They accepted the gift and the Flying Buddies were so glad about it that they would have liked to do a highland fling. A bit later, the Gonzalas sailed off in a plane for Cuzco, and as long as the machine remained in sight, they could see the brothers and the woman waving happily.

"O migosh, do the De Castros know we are alive?" Jim asked.

"They do, and they do not know that their plane was smashed. We have sent one to replace it. The Don said to do that and it will save no end of explanations," Bob answered.

"Well, then, that's that—oh," he turned to Ynilea—"Do you know anything about that platinum deposit that started all this rumpus?"

"A little. We have a place where it is

washed. Can you guess what we did when it was discovered?"

"Let me see—did you get it away, or cover it over?"

"Bet I can guess," Bob chuckled. "You made a dry fork out of a wet one by switching the streams about. Don't you remember, old man, the irrigating system, and all that, you know, these fellows were masters of water supply when Moses took to the bullrushes."

"Great guns," Jim laughed. "Of course, well—"

"We will now join Mr. Austin in the chorus of the national anthem of Siam," Bob shouted.

THE END